"What if I woke you by whispering something suggestive in your ear?"

A throaty hum vibrated through Josie as if to agree. Keith's body heated instantly in response, feeling a definite sexual connection to this woman who hadn't even opened her eyes. Could she be starting to wake up? Liking what he had to say?

The possibility tantalized him.

"I'm damn attracted to you," he said, letting the words sink in, half hoping she'd throw herself into his arms.

"I'm seriously restraining myself from touching you right now." Still, no reply. No flutter of her lashes or shifting in sleep. "I'd like nothing better than to peel off your clothes inch by inch with my teeth."

He could see that she was still dozing, yet a slow, sexy smile curved her lips. He could hardly believe his eyes. But then she moaned softly in her sleep, moving her palm down her throat and under the fabric of her collar, cupping her breast as her tongue darted out to wet her lower lip.

Holy. Hell.

Heat shot to his groin in a rush so forceful it was damn near painful.

Whatever he was doing, it was working...

Blaze

Dear Reader,

One of the great joys in writing is seeing what characters stroll onto the page. Often, I work hard to develop and get to know characters before I begin a book. I created the Murphy brothers that way, thinking of them as a group. But some of their heroines surprised me. Like Josie Passano. Josie arrived fully formed and ready for her story, seemingly with no effort on my part. You've got to love it when that happens.

I hope you'll enjoy Josie's accidental meeting with sexy entrepreneur Keith Murphy, and keep your eye on some of Keith's brothers as they make their appearances. You'll be meeting more of them throughout 2012, since the guys all captured my heart and my imagination. The Murphy brothers were a vocal, rowdy crew and I could hardly say no when they came courting.

Thanks so much for reading, and don't forget to check out my website, www.joannerock.com, for a contest every month to win free books and more.

Happy reading,

Joanne Rock

Joanne Rock

RIDING THE STORM

TORONTO NEW YORK LONDON
AMSTERDAM PARIS SYDNEY HAMBURG
STOCKHOLM ATHENS TOKYO MILAN MADRID
PRAGUE WARSAW BUDAPEST AUCKLAND

Recycling programs
for this product may
not exist in your area.

ISBN-13: 978-0-373-79647-2

RIDING THE STORM

ABOUT THE AUTHOR

The mother of three sports-minded sons, Joanne Rock's primary occupation is carting kids to practices and cheering on their athletic prowess at any number of sporting events. In the windows of time between football games, she loves to write and cheer on happily-ever-afters. A three-time RITA® Award nominee, Joanne is the author of more than fifty books for a variety of Harlequin series. She has been an *RT Book Reviews* Career Achievement Award nominee and multiple Reviewers' Choice finalist, including a nomination for *The Captive* (Blaze #534) as Best Blaze of 2010. Her work has been reprinted in twenty-six countries and translated into nineteen languages. Over two million copies of her books are in print. For more information on Joanne's books, visit www.joannerock.com.

Books by Joanne Rock

To Dean,
no stranger to weathering the occasional storm.

1

Chatham, Massachusetts

ONE DAY, Josie Passano would be a world-famous interior decorator, and she would hire a personal driver. Then she would have someone to guide her around dark marinas at midnight to meet with clients who were too busy to see her at a reasonable hour.

Stepping carefully along the planked pier with boats tied up on both sides, she was grateful she'd at least thought to wear flats instead of the heels she normally preferred for client meetings. At five foot three, she liked the height and sense of presence a pair of heels could give her—probably a holdover from her days as a fashion designer. Of course, that was before all hell had broken loose in her former career. But tonight, under an inky sky, with waves splashing up onto the dock, wearing heels would have landed her at the bottom of the Atlantic for sure.

"Slip number thirty-nine, which one are you?" Shiv-

ering in the cooling late-summer air, Josie squinted at
the tiny numbers etched into stone slab markers near
the boats. She wished there were some signs of life on
one of the decks so she could ask someone. How could
she tell which watercraft went with which slip when
there was a sailboat between thirty-seven and thirty-
nine, plus a sailboat between thirty-nine and forty-one,
but none directly in front of the markers?

With nothing to suggest one direction or the other,
Josie tugged her cell phone out of her pocket and called
her client, Wall Street bigwig Chase Freeman, for input
on his boat's whereabouts.

"Chase, I'm standing between slip thirty-seven and
thirty-nine and having a devil of a time figuring out
which boat is yours." She peered around the docks,
wishing the marina office was still open. "Can you call
me back?"

Chase had requested a meeting on the vessel she
hoped to decorate to fatten up her interior-design portfolio. They were distantly related—he was someone she
saw at family wakes and weddings—but she'd never
particularly cared for him. He'd acted as if he was doing
her a big favor while being difficult about agreeing on a
time to meet. But she'd persevered because she needed
the account, and it wasn't as if her packed schedule presented her with many openings, either.

By the time all was said and done, he'd insisted
he couldn't do the meeting any other time but after a
friend's engagement party in Chatham, name-dropping
that the shindig was for Ryan Murphy. The Murphys

were a well-known, mega-rich Cape Cod family, and the oldest son's engagement had been in the society papers in Boston, where her business was based. These days, Josie only read those papers to search for potential clients. She still held a grudge against the tabloids after they'd raked her over the coals for being a "party girl" when she was younger and circulating socially to promote her work in fashion. She'd put the fallout from those days to rest when she'd changed her name and left New York City. But she was still keeping that world at arm's length while she got her new business off the ground.

Anyway, Chase had yammered on and on about his travel schedule and a trip to Singapore, trying to impress her at every turn with his access to millions. Whatever. A big bank account didn't make you any cooler, in Josie's book—a message she'd been trying to send her overprivileged parents ever since she was about ten. But Chase had a serious budget for this project, and as a struggling solo designer trying to break out onto the next level, she needed this kind of account. Decorating a boat interior would be something unique to add to her design portfolio before she pitched a do-it-yourself show to a Boston-based cable company.

Hello, new audience. Between her new name and location, it would take a little while before anyone made the connection to the scandal of her past. And by then, with any luck, her business and the show would have enough momentum to weather the inevitable media storm.

But first she had to work her tail off to get to that spot of unassailable success. Like now, when she was so exhausted from an open house in Yarmouth this morning that she could hardly put one foot in front of the other, let alone figure out which boat went with these cursed slip signs.

"This has to be it," she muttered to herself, tired of staring back and forth between slip thirty-seven and thirty-nine. The boat closest to her had a light on, and wouldn't that make sense for a man who expected company?

Decision made, she called Marlena.

"Josie, please say you arrived in one piece?" Her assistant, a college intern who'd stayed on after the internship was complete, launched right into conversation. "You sounded exhausted while you were driving."

"I'm here. And it's too late for you to be working, by the way." Josie shifted a bag full of design inspiration books to her other shoulder, glad to hear Marlena's voice. It was great to have help back at the office while she was out on the road.

"You're a fine one to talk. You set a terrible example for me, working constantly. Have you ever taken a vacation in your whole life?"

Josie grinned, far preferring this vision of herself to the one she'd grown up with—that you were only a success if you didn't *have* to work.

"I don't mean to be a bad role model. I just like the job."

"Me, too," Marlena replied. "That doesn't mean I can do it successfully if I'm at it eighteen hours a day."

"Heard and understood." Josie knew she would probably benefit from a little downtime. Maybe next year. In the meanwhile, she appreciated her assistant's candor—as well as the work ethic that mirrored her own. "Have I thanked you lately for being my assistant?"

"Yes. Have I thanked you lately for treating me like a creative contributor and not a peon intern who can only fetch your coffee?" Marlena spoke loudly over the harpsichord music she favored whenever she sketched design ideas. "You're going places, J.P. I hitched my wagon to a rising star."

"Yes, well, I certainly hope so. But I wish I could have arrived here earlier. I had every intention of being on-site before sunset so I could look over the space in the daylight, but I got talking to that journalist at the open house." She'd been delayed by a woman from the local press who wanted to feature the historic home in Yarmouth in an upcoming style section.

While Josie talked, she stepped aboard the large, lit deck of the sleek boat in slip thirty-nine.

"Right. I sent her those photos you asked me about." Marlena turned down her music. "Will you call me when you finish up with Freeman?"

"No way." Josie walked carefully in case the deck was slippery, her eye on the stairs leading below deck, where it might be warmer. "You put in more hours than I pay you for already. I'll text you afterward and we'll talk in the morning, okay?"

"Deal. Good luck, J.P."

Disconnecting, Josie used the light on her cell phone to help illuminate a path to the covered section of the deck near what was obviously the control center for the vessel, complete with a radio and a couple of readout screens.

Still chilly from the cool air blowing off the waves, she hoped it was okay to seek a warmer part of the boat while she waited. Gingerly, she made her way down a couple narrow steps into the kitchen, where a low-wattage light over the countertop helped her find her way around. The boat was simple and somewhat austere, designwise. Functional, she supposed. She quite liked the vibe and found herself vaguely surprised that Mr. Moneybags owned something so understated. But then, he'd hired her to redo it, hadn't he? He probably wanted to deck the thing out in designer silks and mahogany. She didn't see any note from Chase inviting her to make herself at home, but then, thoughtfulness had never been his strong suit. At the last family reunion, she'd seen him texting under the table while halfheartedly engaged in a conversation with his great-aunt.

Josie found a couple wooden benches on either side of a small table, and promptly dropped her swatch books and inspiration pictures on one of the built-in seats. The cabin area remained dim even with some of the exterior deck light filtering through the high windows. Josie slid onto the seat beside her gear and promptly lurched forward, thanks to a particularly forceful wave.

Her stomach rolled in response.

Damn it. She hated to give in and take the motion-sickness meds she'd stashed in her purse, especially since she was already tired and the drug could make her drowsier. But while she hadn't been on a boat since she was seven or eight years old, she'd spent that short cruise to Catalina turning green and begging for the ride to be over. Drowsiness was preferable to tossing her cookies on Chase's shoes. Although chances were good he might deserve it, she needed this job too much to risk upsetting her client.

Popping two pills to be safe, Josie tugged out her swatch books and pictures, looking through them for design ideas to spruce up the vintage sailboat interior. She wanted to have some suggestions ready when Chase walked in, so they could sign the contract and be done for the night. The last thing she wanted to do was fall asleep while she waited.

But after forcing her eyes over the same line of copy and piece of ivory-colored sailcloth about ten times, Josie realized she was more exhausted than she'd re-alized. With little sleep the night before, prepping for today's open house, and lots of mingling with potential clients and guests from the press corps, followed by the drive to Chatham in the dark, she was wiped out. Good thing she had no personal life to speak of, or she'd never be able to keep up this pace.

Personal life. Ha! She didn't even want to think about how long it'd been since she'd indulged in that ultimate de-stressor—hot, sweaty, fabulous sex. Scandal had erupted for her three years earlier when she'd been photographed kissing a congressman who'd never told her he was married. And the ensuing media frenzy had been a dropkick to her libido. Every photo of her ever taken had surfaced—from the nights she'd trolled expensive clubs in her original designs to drum up interest in her work, to her teenage years, when she'd been a brat with too much money and privilege, flipping off paparazzi while shopping in Milan, or dancing in a public fountain in Amsterdam with a beer in hand. With all the negative publicity, Josie had made the decision to cut herself off from her family's fortune. She'd started over from scratch, reinventing herself completely.

The move had been a healthy one, and she thrived in her new field. But she hadn't found time to resurrect the sex life she'd left behind with the rest of her past....

Shoving aside vague memories of intimacy from the years before she'd started her interior design business, Josie decided maybe she would be fresher for the meeting with Chase if she took the tiniest catnap. Clearly, the medicine was kicking in and giving the one-two punch to her already exhausted body.

She propped her chin on her hand and told herself she'd close her eyes only for a moment. She would hear Chase when he came on board, and be awake before he could walk down the stairs.

It was her last conscious thought before she succumbed to the delicious luxury of sleep, sweetened with a dream that brought a smile to her lips.

KEITH MURPHY WAS NONE too happy to see Chase Freeman's big-ass boat parked too close to the *Vesta,* a twenty-six-foot Pearson Triton he'd just agreed to sail down to Charleston for his brother.

Scowling at the flashy, thirty-foot Nonsuch Ultra nosing well into the neighboring slip, Keith hoped he'd be able to back out of the marina without hitting the other boat. He needed to get under way, make some serious progress toward South Carolina, before his brother Jack caught on to the prank Keith had pulled at their oldest brother, Ryan's, engagement party tonight. While toasting the future bridegroom on the lawn of the Murphy family compound, Keith had deliberately baited Jack.

It hadn't taken much, since his second oldest brother was touchy as hell, and all the Murphys were notoriously competitive. Soon, Jack was taunting Keith back, saying that he couldn't sail his way out of a paper bag. Keith had suggested swapping boats, ostensibly to prove he knew how to sail as well as any of his brothers. His bigger motive had been to get Jack onto his boat—a slick forty-five-foot power catamaran that was too cushy for Jack the purist, but which currently played host to Jack's ex-girlfriend. And Jack had fallen for the bait and switch so damn easily. Right now, he was probably halfway to Bar Harbor, Maine, to deliver the catamaran to Keith's chief financial officer. Jack would get one hell of a surprise when he discovered Alicia on board, sleeping peacefully in anticipation of a lift to Bar Harbor from Keith.

Of course, all Keith's matchmaking efforts were purely to benefit Jack.

As CEO of Green Principles, an environmentally minded company he'd grown from the ground up, Keith had worked his butt off this summer on a merger with a competing firm. He had finally acquired the company two weeks ago, and he needed a break before his next major project—to cement a partnership with Wholesome Branding, a global marketer that could take Green Principles to an international level by recommending it to companies that needed a "greener" image. Green Principles helped businesses and corporations of all sizes to become more environmentally friendly. They assessed a client's carbon footprint, paper waste, recycling efforts and energy use, highlighting problem areas and making suggestions for improvement, projecting costs for the changes and putting the clients in touch with contractors and suppliers who could implement them.

Sailing south in a vintage Pearson Triton for a few days sounded like the perfect way to clear his head from one deal and strategize how to manage the next. In Charleston, Keith would hand off the boat to Jack's friend, who was supposed to buy the vessel. By the time Keith came home, he'd be recharged and ready to make the partnership with Wholesome Branding work.

Assuming he could maneuver around that damn Nonsuch butting into his space.

Cursing the big shot Wall Street broker who'd attended the family engagement party, Keith climbed onto Jack's trim, highly functional sailboat. Sizewise, it wasn't that much smaller than Chase Freeman's ride. But everything about the *Vesta* seemed sleeker. Keith would figure out how to get her under way without any help from the owner of the boat next door. Last he'd seen Freeman at the party, the guy had been feeling no pain on the dance floor. He didn't look as if he intended to head back to his boat for the night anytime soon.

Keith loosened his tie, then thought better of it and whipped the silk right off his neck. He tossed it aside, not caring where the thing fell. His responsibilities were done as of now.

For a moment, he debated scouting around below deck for some boat shoes or a pair of jeans. But considering his haste to get out of Dodge before his brother realized what he'd done, he settled for bare feet and rolling up his trousers. He switched on the motor for close maneuvering—sails and rigging could wait until he had more room to work. Already Keith could feel anticipation firing through him. Much as he enjoyed the perks of the corporate power cat, and all the bells and whistles of GPS position locking and docking, he had grown up on Cape Cod and he loved to sail. It was in the Murphy blood.

Two hours later, he had the *Vesta* out in the open water.

The night air was cool and crisp. He'd ditched his dinner jacket long ago, after sprinting forward and aft a few times to make adjustments on the sails. Even though he had ideal conditions—the weather showed he could sail on a reach for at least the next day or two if he could stay ahead of an oncoming storm system—he'd bungled the jib and had a close call with the boom in his haste to get to sea. Now, he had a beauty of a draft going as the boat cut through the water with ease. His navigation lights cast warring patterns of green and red on the deck, while all around him the sea grew darker as he left Cape Cod in the distance. Traffic heading north, toward Boston, would be heavy in the morning. But right now, he had the water to himself. He avoided the shipping lanes, steering clear of bigger vessels.

Tempted to pound his chest and roar with the sense of accomplishment, Keith did exactly that. He let out a howl for good measure. His ex-navy brother had been talking trash to say Keith had forgotten how to sail. Just because his work had kept him busy the last couple of years didn't mean he'd gone soft.

He took advantage of the favorable wind for another hour before he called it a night, tucking into quiet waters off Nantucket to anchor. By now, he'd left Chatham far enough behind that his brother couldn't call off their deal to exchange boats. Besides, exhaustion was kicking in, and Keith still had to secure the sheets and rigging for the night.

It was going on 4:00 a.m. by the time he stumbled down the steps in the companionway.

And damn near had a heart attack.

He could see the shadowed outline of a figure—a woman, slumped over the table in the middle of the main salon. She had her head cradled on her arms atop a huge, open book. Through a veil of dark hair, he could just make out the pale skin of her cheek.

"Miss?" he called stupidly. But his heart raced with the fear that she was injured, or worse.

If she was alive and breathing, how could she have slept through three hours at sea?

Shoving past some built-in storage bins, he knelt beside her to feel for a pulse, already wondering how in the hell he would explain to the police why he'd left without checking over the boat. But—thank you, God— her heartbeat thrummed softly against his thumb where he gripped her wrist. A wave of relief flooded through his veins, so hard and fast that he sank onto the seat beside her. Too soon, other worries crowded his brain. Did she have a medical condition, or need some kind of emergency attention?

And what the hell was she doing on Jack's boat in the middle of the night?

He tugged his cell phone out of his pants pocket, only to discover he had no service. No surprise, really, this far off the coast of Nantucket. He'd dropped anchor in shallow waters but hadn't sailed too far in, so that he'd be able to get under way faster after sunrise.

Calling to mind some half-forgotten CPR class he'd taken during a summer of lifeguarding on a Cape Cod beach, Keith tried to take a reasonable inventory of the woman's vital signs. She breathed evenly. Wasn't feverish. Heart rate normal for an adult female at rest. And hello, was she ever female. While widening her collar for better access to the pulse at her neck, he got an eyeful of black lace bra cups beneath her soft blouse.

If he'd still feared for her health, he might not have noticed. Well, he certainly wouldn't have noticed in such *detail*. But with the worst of his fears assuaged by a quick check, his normal male instincts kicked back in with a vengeance. This woman—lying on a book of fabric swatches, he discovered—was a looker.

Shoulder-length dark hair framed delicate features in a heart-shaped face. Her slender nose tilted gently upward above lips that were deep pink, even without makeup. Long, beaded earrings tangled in her hair, and he realized her whole outfit was vaguely artsy. She wore faux snakeskin shoes and baggy jeans rolled up slightly to show off her ankles. Her dark peasant blouse was densely embroidered, underneath a more austere black jacket. A series of silver necklaces dipped into the generous cleavage he continued to admire. For a petite woman—under five and a half feet, for sure—she carried just the right amount of curves.

Shifting on the bench seat beside her, he touched her cheek. Not just because he wanted to, but because he really needed to wake her up. Had she been a guest who'd imbibed too much at his brother's engagement party?

She wasn't really dressed for a semiformal shindig, and he had the feeling he would have noticed her if she'd been in attendance. Women hadn't been on his radar lately, but this one? She made the grade with her eyes closed. Literally.

He was surprised when she answered his touch with a throaty hum.

In fact, the low, feminine vibration seemed to electrify his whole hand, the pulse surging pleasantly through his skin.

"Miss?" He brushed his thumb along the top of her cheekbone. "Are you all right?"

She turned sleepily toward him, another incoherent murmur on her lips. Her shoulders rolled with the movement, as if she had an ache in her neck. Her shifting clothes released a hint of perfume, something vanilla laden and sexy that made him want to lean in and inhale deeply.

He told himself to ease his hand away. The dim salon of the gently rocking boat suddenly felt too intimate. He didn't want to frighten her when she awoke. But forcing his fingers from that warm, silky skin was another matter altogether. It had been many months since he'd last held a woman. And even that—a passing encounter with an ex—had been a brief release in a work-intensive year.

"Who are you?" he asked, the feel of her still warming his palm even after he moved his hand to the table.

He peered past her to the stack of heavy books on the other side of the bench they shared.

"You've got to be a designer of some kind, right?"

But despite the evidence of her career calling, he could hardly picture his brother hiring anyone to redecorate the *Vesta*. Jack had no style—or if he did,

Keith would call it Spartan, at best. So what would this woman be doing on his boat in the middle of the night?

"There's no way Jack is involved with someone," he mused aloud, hoping the sound of his voice would wake her up.

Keith knew his brother was still hung up on Alicia. He definitely wouldn't be hooking up with a stranger at midnight after a family party. Besides, the woman next to Keith hadn't come to the *Vesta* for a tryst or she wouldn't have brought her decorating books.

"Which means you're fair game." He double-checked her left hand for a ring even as he made the pronouncement. "There's no reason I can't flirt with you. I've been a perfect gentleman."

No reasonable person could hold the glance at her breasts against him, right? He'd been scared for her life; that was his story and he was sticking to it. Because this woman—whoever she was—had him gaping as if he'd never seen a female before.

Sighing in her sleep, she brushed a strand of hair from her face, her fingers ending up near the pale column of her throat, exactly where he'd like to touch her. His awareness shifted into overdrive, his body responding instantly.

"Maybe too much of a gentleman," he continued, his own fingers itching for the slightest excuse to return to her skin. "*You're* passed out on *my* boat—well, my boat for the next week, anyway. Who would blame me if I woke you up by whispering something suggestive in your ear?"

Maybe he could plant in her sleeping brain a few torrid notions she'd be anxious to act on when she opened her eyes. He knew a thing or two about the power of suggestion. He'd studied some business psychology, after all.

Another throaty hum vibrated through her as if she agreed. His body heated in response, feeling a definite sexual connection to this woman who hadn't even opened her eyes. Could she be starting to wake up? Liking what he had to say?

The possibility was tantalizing.

"You're going to be wildly attracted to me when you come to," he told her. "Wait a minute. You're not hypnotized. You're just sleeping." He didn't have any power over her subconscious and he didn't want to tick her off by coming on too strong. "How about this—I'm damn attracted to you."

He let that sink in, half hoping she'd throw herself into his arms. Hey, it could happen.

"I'm seriously restraining myself from touching you right now." Still no reply. No flutter of her lashes or sexy shifting in her sleep. "I'd like nothing better than to peel your clothes off inch by inch with my teeth."

A slow, sexy smile curved her lips. He could hardly believe his eyes. But then she moaned softly in her sleep, moving her palm down her throat and under the fabric of her collar, cupping her breast as her tongue darted out to wet her lower lip.

Holy. Hell.

Heat shot to his groin in a rush so forceful it was damn near painful.

Whatever he was doing, it was working.

2

JOSIE COULDN'T REMEMBER the last time she'd had such a nice dream.

Usually, she woke up instantly to her alarm clock, bouncing out of bed with no memory of her nighttime imaginings. But right now she reveled in the groggy half sleep that left her body relaxed and her mind free to wander. It was a delicious, self-indulgent feeling to simply lie there. Josie felt better than peaceful. She felt…warm all over. Her skin hummed, vibrant and alive. Awareness sparked along her nerve endings, tingling sweetly in all the best places.

From somewhere in the deep recesses of her brain, a man's voice resonated.

"I can't wait to taste you." The low, confident tone did wicked things to her already simmering libido.

Her breasts beaded at the thought of the dream man's mouth on her. She arched toward the sound, a wordless plea for him to make good on the sensual threat.

When he didn't comply immediately, she knew a moment's frustration. She wanted to draw him closer, to feel his tongue on her breast, licking away the hungry tension in skin that felt too tight. Too needy. But her limbs were heavy and lethargic.

"Please," she murmured, her fingers sliding over her taut nipple. "Please."

She could almost feel the warm breath of her fantasy man on her skin there, right where she wanted him. His scent, clean and salty like an ocean breeze, teased her nose.

Needing him, she drew her hand from her blouse and flung her arm forward. The movement jarred her, causing an ache in her neck. Her head fell off her pillow onto a cold, hard surface that wasn't her bed.

Confused, Josie struggled to return to a comfortable spot. To the sweet lure of her fantasy man and a dream that felt incredibly real.

"Are you okay?" the deep bass voice asked.

Damn it. Why wasn't he asking her to unbutton her blouse? To slide beneath silk sheets with him and tear off all their clothes?

She waited for her consciousness to return to that sexy, dreamy place. Instead, the ache in her neck increased.

"Wake up, beautiful," the man in her dreams said.

But oddly, his voice seemed clearer now. Closer, somehow.

Wrenching her heavy eyelids open, Josie forced herself to take stock of her surroundings. To figure out why her pillow was so hard. To see why her alarm hadn't gone off and why she was lazing around in the dark....

"Oh, my God," she whispered.

A real, live, hot-looking man sat beside her in a room lit by a green, wavering night-light. He wore a light-colored dress shirt unbuttoned to the middle of his chest, exposing strong, well-defined pecs beneath. A silver saint's medallion hung around his neck.

She didn't recognize him. Could never have met him before this moment or she would have remembered. His chiseled jaw was covered with a shadow of late-night bristles. Full, sculpted lips; a straight Roman nose. Eyes an uncommon color, though it was too dark to tell the shade for sure. Green, maybe? Dark eyelashes framed them and heavy eyebrows topped them. An old scar ran across his forehead.

Details that were way too real for a dream.

"What are you doing here?" She straightened quickly, making herself dizzy. A spike of adrenaline pierced the sensual awareness that had held her captive a moment ago. "Where am I?"

Her pulse raced as she tried to absorb her surroundings. The stranger with her. Just because he was absurdly handsome didn't exclude the possibility that he meant her harm.

"You're on my brother's boat. The *Vesta*." He spoke slowly and calmly, his tone soothing her where it had once stoked a fire inside her. "You must have boarded it last night when it was still docked in Chatham."

"Chatham?" Her heart rate slowed a little at his reasonable tone of voice. His presence wasn't threatening even though he sat close beside her inside… "A boat?"

Realization hit her like a cartoon anvil to the head.

"The boat!" she exclaimed, remembering her trip to Chatham. She latched on to the swatch book on the table in front of her. "I boarded the boat to discuss some new designs for my cousin Chase…" The horror of the moment began to dawn on her. "Oh, God. You're not Chase Freeman."

"No." The sexy stranger shook his head as he took a document out of his wallet and passed it to her. "I'm Keith Murphy, and my boat was docked beside his." The document proved to be his driver's license, which confirmed his claim and his residence in Chatham. "Maybe you wandered onto the wrong vessel?"

She'd completely missed her appointment with Chase the night before.

"Oh no." Her stomach sank as full alertness returned. She remembered being exhausted and worried about getting seasick. "The numbering on the slips was so confusing. I thought this was the right boat because the lights were on. Then I took some motion sickness medicine and it must have knocked me out. What time is it?"

Maybe she could still meet Chase. Rising to her feet, she tried to pull herself together until the man—Keith— gently grasped her wrist.

"It's four in the morning and we're not in Chatham anymore. I didn't know you were on board and I set sail about one o'clock."

She found it tough to focus on his words when he squeezed, then released her. How could a total stranger's touch feel so familiar? So incredibly good?

Snippets of her sexy dream returned to her and she wondered...

"Did anything else happen while I was sleeping?" Sinking back onto the seat beside him, she tried to process the situation. Her skin buzzed with a palpable, electric hum. "That is, did we..."

She had no idea where she was going with that question. But her nerve endings vibrated with keen awareness. He had said things to her, sexy things, hadn't he? Her heartbeat quickened at the blur of steamy memories.

Mr. Fantasy smiled a thousand-watt grin that was sexy and shameless. "You were out of it when I got down here, but you didn't talk in your sleep or anything, if that's what you're worried about."

"Not really. I..." How could she explain that she felt as turned on as if he'd touched her? That she was kind of worried she'd thrown herself at him in her half-dreaming state?

She smoothed a hand over her hair, trying to restore some order and some self control. This wasn't like her at all.

"Look, Miss..." He seemed to be waiting for her to fill in the blank.

"Oh. Josie Passano." She extended her hand. "I apologize for boarding the wrong boat. If we could just turn around, I could try to salvage my meeting. I really needed that account."

"Josie." He tested the name and seemed to like it, if his slow nod was any indication. "Can I get you something to drink first?"

Rising, he flicked on a low light over the galley cooktop, making her realize they'd been sitting in the green glow of a night-light all that time. Good heavens, she was out of it. The medicine must have done a number on her.

"That would be great. Cold water, if you have any."

As he moved toward the small icebox, she noticed his shirttails were untucked and his feet were bare. He'd rolled up his trousers like a man who'd just waded in the ocean. She liked that he'd kept some distance as she woke up, his smooth, deep voice and relaxed body language all putting her at ease when she had every right to be scared to death to find herself on a stranger's boat in the middle of the night.

He turned and caught her staring.

"Here you go." Offering her a clear plastic cup, he filled a second for himself and sat across from her at the small table. "Josie, I doubt that Chase Freeman made it back to his boat last night, so I wouldn't worry about him remembering a missed appointment until afternoon at the earliest. I saw him on the dance floor at my brother's engagement party and he looked like he'd had a few too many. I'd be willing to bet he either crashed at my parents' place or at a, uh, friend's house."

She read between the lines that her cousin had been

trying to hook up with someone. Not that she cared about his personal life other than how it affected their business relationship. What threw her for a loop was connecting the dots that this man—Mr. Fantasy—was a Murphy. He'd said it, but she hadn't fully appreciated the import.

She hoped he didn't know her train wreck of a family. Thankfully, her name change had given her the anonymity she craved.

"Robert Murphy is your father?" She straightened in her seat, wishing she hadn't shown up on the wrong boat like some sex-starved Goldilocks, all hot and bothered for her host.

She must look completely unprofessional, darn it. Didn't she always tell Marlena you never knew where you might meet your next client? If she were on her game, she might be able to talk her way into a meeting with a representative of Murphy Resorts. But that wasn't going to happen if she kept drooling over Keith.

And his well-connected family was all the more reason not to get involved. She had no desire to land back in Boston's society columns, having her private life dissected. For that matter, after how kind he'd been to her, she wouldn't want to foist bad press on Keith, either.

"Yes. He and my mom hosted a big party for my brother and his fiancée last night. That's why the marina was so crowded. A lot of the guests came by boat." He sipped his water, watching her over the rim of his cup.

"You said you took motion-sickness medicine. How are you doing now that it's worn off?"

"Me?" She hadn't given it a second thought, but she'd been so fuzzy headed since waking up, her gray matter wasn't working at full speed. "Fine, I think. I might have been hasty with the Dramamine. I got seasick on a boat ride to Catalina when I was young, but my mom told me afterward I'd had an ear infection or something." She spoke quickly, nervous now that she realized her host was from one of Boston's top entrepreneurial families. "I took the medicine to be safe, but I think I'd rather brave out the time on your boat and see how it goes, rather than fall asleep again. I can't believe I slept through you coming on board and setting sail. You said we're not in Chatham anymore?"

"We're close to Nantucket." He pointed toward a forgotten swatch sample catalog under her elbow. "May I?"

His hand hovered deliciously close to her arm. For a moment, she thought he was asking for permission to touch her. Warmth swirled in her veins even as she realized he wanted to see her book.

"Of course!" She slid the heavy volume across the table, wondering if he meant to keep her off balance with this conversation. "Nantucket?"

How on earth would she get home? She'd have to take a plane or a ferry. She'd lose a whole day's work because she'd stepped onto the wrong boat last night. Then again, was Keith Murphy interested in redecorating? Maybe she could salvage a job, at least.

"Yes." He opened the book as smoothly as if he was in a boardroom on a business lunch and not chatting up a stowaway on his sailboat at four in the morning. "I'm taking the *Vesta* down to Charleston to sell it for my brother Jack."

Josie tried to absorb that. Apparently, when you were a Murphy, you did things like that—sail boats around to sell them because you were so rich you could probably buy five more you liked better. She pictured her parents giving their wholehearted approval to Keith.

Not that she was thinking about dating him or anything. That would be a disaster waiting to happen, given his high-profile family. Besides, her parents' stamp of approval was a dubious endorsement at best. She respected people who *worked* for their income.

"Well, I don't want to hold you up or anything, but I should find my way back to the mainland before you head any farther south." Even though this evening had been interesting, to say the least. Even though she still had the sense that something had happened between her and Keith before she awoke. Why else had she felt so turned on and twitchy when she opened her eyes?

"Of course." He fingered a square of handmade Thai silk in her swatch book. "But would you mind waiting until daylight? I already furled the sails for the night and we're far enough away from the mainland that it would take too long to motor in. After sailing single-handed for three hours and doing the family party before that, I've gotta say I'm beat."

"Oh." How awkward. "I'm sure you are tired. I can just…wait until you're ready."

She had a vision of herself watching him sleep, quickly followed by an even more rewarding vision of her tiring him out thoroughly so he could sleep even better. Mmm.

"But I don't want you to feel uncomfortable. We can radio in to the Coast Guard if it would make you more at ease about being out here with me." He closed the book and met her gaze over the tabletop.

Green, she thought idly. His eyes were an unusual shade of golden-green. As she stared back at him, half-hypnotized by the leftover effects of her medicine and the vague memories of her dreams about him talking to her in her sleep, she felt heat crawl over her skin again. Warming her everywhere. Making her all too aware of Keith Murphy.

And keenly aware of how long it had been since she'd been with a man. Maybe if you suppressed your sex drive long enough, it took vengeance on you by going rogue at the sight of a hot guy. That would explain her fear that she'd launch herself onto him at any moment.

"That's thoughtful of you, and I would appreciate it." She focused on her words instead of her feelings, needing to maintain professional distance. "I was nervous about meeting a client on a strange boat at midnight anyhow, so I left messages with a few friends. They'll be worried about me, since I never checked in again."

He led her out of the salon toward the helm, where the radio equipment was housed. When they reached the companionway, which was slick with seawater, he extended an arm to steady her.

As Josie placed her palm on his strong forearm, she had the strangest sense this wasn't the first time they'd touched. And even though her attraction to Keith was unwise, to say the least, she couldn't help but wish it wouldn't be the last time she'd feel him against her.

KEITH HAD FORMED a multimillion-dollar corporation on the strength of his people skills. But he'd never been more grateful for his one-on-one communication abilities than right here, right now.

Interior designer Josie Passano had the face of an angel, plus a wicked glint in her brown eyes, as if she were thinking about something altogether interesting. And Keith wanted to know her much, much better. But given their awkward introduction and the iffy proposition of spending the night on the boat together, he planned to play it safe until she felt more comfortable around him. Her reaction to him while she was sleeping gave him hope she wasn't immune. But if he came on too strong now—when they were isolated in the middle of the Atlantic—she'd have every reason to be nervous. It'd be different if they'd met on dry land and he just wanted another date. Convincing her to sail down the coast with him for a little while presented a unique challenge, yet he was up for the task.

He had a few ideas for how to keep her around a little longer, but they all hinged on him not looking as if he was trying too hard. Lucky for him, he was taking his first vacation in years. There couldn't be a better time to pencil in an affair—the first for him since he broke up with family friend Brooke Blaylock a year ago. Brooke's insistence on being the life of the party at all times, causing a stir wherever she went, had been fun for a while. But his patience with the party crowd had worn thin—he was trying to build a business. Besides, he wanted clients to recognize his face from the business section, not the society pages.

Obviously, he was over Brooke by now. And more than ready to move on.

After they got in touch with the Coast Guard, he convinced Josie to take the berth in the front of the boat, while he slept in a bunk in the main salon. He hadn't been lying about being exhausted, so she didn't have to worry about him whispering suggestive ideas in her ear while she slept this time. Not that he wouldn't be dreaming about doing those things to her.

"There should be spare toothbrushes in the bathroom cabinet," he told her as he scrounged up clean towels and fresh sheets for the bed in the boat's only true cabin. "My mom didn't blink at the sight of blood or the regular trips to the E.R. that came with having five kids and a foster son, but she would have a conniption if we didn't floss."

Keith didn't know where that odd bit of Murphy family lore had come from, but he was so tired he seemed to be running on autopilot.

"I'll be fine," Josie assured him, clutching the folded blue T-shirt he'd found for her to sleep in. "Thank you for helping me get in touch with the Coast Guard. My friends will sleep better knowing I wasn't tossed overboard last night."

The radio operator had been kind enough to text Josie's assistant, even though it was above and beyond his duty. The guy had assured them it was a quiet night on his watch and he didn't mind.

"Not a problem. You sure you're feeling okay? No seasickness?" He'd been keeping an eye on her ever since she woke up, knowing the symptoms could come on quickly. But her color seemed good.

Everything about her, for that matter, seemed great. He liked her sexy dark eyes and the mischievous twist to her lips. He definitely liked the confident way she walked and the graceful way she moved. He couldn't take his eyes off her.

"I feel steady." She nodded as if to reassure him, and he realized it was his cue to leave. "I think the uneasy feeling earlier was just a by-product of exhaustion."

His feet remained glued to the floor in the doorway. Damn, but he was usually more polished than this. He had a rep as the Murphy family charmer—the one who could talk anyone into anything. That skill had gotten him far in business, and it usually came through with women, as well. Why did smooth words elude him with Josie?

"I know this has been an unorthodox way to meet," he started, going off script and surprising himself with words he hadn't carefully prepared in his head first. "But it's nice to know you, Josie Passano."

He lingered, his eyes roving over her even when he'd instructed them not to. Where the hell were his people skills?

She grinned, dazzling him more than a little with the warmth of that smile.

"Nice to meet you, too, Keith." Her head tipped to one side as she started to close the door, peeking out at him until the last moment. "Sorry to stow away on you like this."

Watching her mouth move, he imagined what her lips would taste like. Vowed he'd find out for himself as soon as possible.

"No worries. As stowaways go, you were a pleasant surprise." He heard his own voice hit a smoky note as he remembered talking to her earlier, while she'd been sleeping. Would his words come back to her tonight when she closed her eyes? "Sweet dreams, Josie."

"You, too. 'Night." Silently, she shut the door, leaving him staring at the barrier between him and the most interesting woman he'd come across in a long time.

In business, he never let any obstacle stand in his way. But what he felt for his unexpected guest was very, very personal. He would respect her boundaries tonight.

Tomorrow?

He had every intention of closing the deal.

3

MAYBE SHE'D READ a few too many romance novels over the years, but Josie couldn't help lingering in the shower the next day, fantasizing provocative scenarios involving stowaways and sexy sea captains.

Didn't the ship captain always insist on stashing his nubile female passenger in his quarters to protect her from his men? Of course, then he had to sleep in the cabin with her to keep an eye on her. Inevitably, he couldn't keep his hands off her—an arrangement that led to page after page of scandalously delicious sex without the judgmental eyes of regular society looking on.

Standing there, with hot water streaming over her skin, Josie was grateful to the twenty-first century for all modern conveniences. But she wouldn't mind a little time travel for the sake of some sensual play with her host. She'd dreamed about him last night, her over-heated imagination conjuring vivid encounters between them. So much so, in fact, she was somewhat nervous about seeing him face-to-face today.

All that stuff she'd dreamed had seemed so real. In theory, she should simply accept her fantasies as a wake-up call to indulge her needs as a female more often, and perhaps work a bit less. That would be the grown-up, well-adjusted-woman's reaction. But who was so well adjusted that she could ignore memories of a hot guy undressing her—inch by slow inch—with his teeth? She suspected she'd blush ten shades of pink when she saw him.

Switching off the water, she reached for a towel and dried herself, wondering how to ignore her unwise interest in Keith. The man surely ran in the same circles as her parents, or at the very least would recognize her family name. Would he know about her scandalous past if she'd introduced herself as Josie Davenport instead of Josie Passano? She'd taken her mother's maiden name after the congressman scandal, glad to formalize her departure from the trust-fund lifestyle that she'd been raised in. She'd stayed out of the society pages for three years while she'd built the new business, letting Marlena attend any work-related events that might attract a tabloid element. The last thing Josie needed was to have her past dragged back out for the world to see before she made her interior design business a success with the regional TV show deal.

And, guaranteed, being seen around New York or Boston with someone like Keith would land her back in the spotlight she needed to avoid.

Yet for the first time in a long time, she didn't feel like making the smart choice professionally. As she put on the navy T-shirt Keith had given her the night before, along with her own jeans, she acknowledged that she wanted to live out all the things she'd dreamed about with him. What her subconscious didn't seem to comprehend was that she *would* find a man to have a fling with, and let off a little steam. Really, she would. But Keith should not be that guy.

She towel dried her hair and dredged up some lip gloss and moisturizer from her purse. When she looked halfway presentable, and wasn't actively fantasizing about Keith's mouth on her…

Whoops.

Trying again to clear her mind, she shoved her other clothes in an empty grocery sack she'd found folded in a bathroom drawer. Taking the sack and her purse with her, she wound her way through the quiet salon and galley toward the companionway, where daylight spilled down into the lower level.

Voices above drew her attention.

"Keith?" she called, stepping up the first stair.

Who could he be speaking to in the middle of the sea? Had the Coast Guard come to check on them after their radio call last night?

"Morning." Keith appeared at the top of the stairs, freshly shaved. Dressed in faded gray cargo shorts and a white polo shirt layered over a white T-shirt, he looked clean and…delicious.

She felt her cheeks warm and knew a blush had colored her skin from the roots of her hair to her neckline. Damn it.

At least she'd gotten it out of the way, right?

"Good morning." Stepping up onto the main deck, she discovered they weren't anchored out in the middle of nowhere anymore. "I see you did some sailing while I was sleeping again."

The boat—the *Vesta,* he'd called it—was already docked on the little island of Nantucket. She'd been there enough times to recognize the south wharf with the rows of gray, cedar-sided cottages lining nearby docks.

Gentle waves rocked their sailboat in time with all the other watercraft in nearby slips. The view, while pretty, made her realize she wouldn't have been any better at discerning one vessel from another in the light of day. Now, if they redid their sails in purple paisley or muted floral chintz, she'd be all set.

And, yikes, didn't that sound like something her mom would say, martini glass in hand as she strolled around the deck?

"I woke up early and figured you would just as soon be docked when you opened your eyes. I pulled into the marina about half an hour ago." He took the bag of clothes and settled it on a seat cushion near the helm.

As a warm breeze lifted her damp hair off her shoulders, she noticed he'd already relocated her design books to the same canvas bolster.

So eager to be rid of her? Disappointment outweighed her relief that a separation would ensure no one resurrected her old scandal by photographing them together.

"Then I won't keep you." She dug in her purse for her business cards. "I'm sure you're anxious to get under way on your trip, and I'm sorry to have slowed you down." Finding the sterling silver case, she handed him a card.

Frowning, he took the cream-colored linen stock bearing the logo that Marlena had designed as one of her first projects as an intern.

"I'm in no hurry." He tucked the card into the pocket of his shorts. "In fact, I'd hoped to buy you breakfast by way of apology for the, uh…accidental kidnapping. I figure if I can bribe you with eggs and sausage, you'll be less likely to press charges."

Pleasure warmed her to her toes while she weighed the probability of anyone recognizing Keith in Nantucket. While she debated the question, a young family pulled a big powerboat into the slip beside them. A boy and a girl—both knee-high and dressed in navy-and-white-striped T-shirts—waved from either side of their mother, while their dad steered the craft into place.

"I *am* hungry," Josie admitted. "But I'm afraid I'm just as guilty as you, since I was the trespasser last night. If anything, I should probably be buying *you* breakfast."

Or dinner, maybe, after an afternoon of acrobatic sex that left them both ravenous. The thought heated her cheeks again, warming her all over in spite of the mild sea breeze. Now why had she said that? Sharing a meal in public with him was a risky proposition at any time. Hadn't she promised herself she was done dating guys who attracted tabloid interest? She had no desire to dredge up her "party-girl" past, after working hard to bury that image.

Although she couldn't help but be miffed that she'd earned the rep without any of the fun it implied. She'd networked her butt off on those nightclub outings, pitching her fashions to the social elite. She'd hoped to catch a few trendy clients who didn't mind taking a risk on a new designer. One of her few impulsive moves during that time had been a kiss in a back alley with a cute guy who'd flirted with her relentlessly. All the other pictures the media had gathered to create the "party-girl" montage had been from her rebellious teenage years, before she'd channeled her energies into productive creativity.

"Hmm. I don't think any judge would see much of a threat in a five-foot trespasser bearing fifty pounds of design swatches." Keith hopped out onto the dock to help the speedboat owner with the young family tie his craft to a cleat. "But how about we debate it over coffee?"

He flashed white teeth, his easy charm drawing her toward him in spite of herself.

"I'm five foot three, actually." Leaving her books behind, she stepped onto the dock, while the kids in the striped shirts and their mom came closer to the bow to watch Keith tie the line. "And I happen to have great aim with a can of Mace, although since I was drugged at the time, I probably didn't pose much danger."

Finishing the knot, Keith reached up to give each of the preschoolers a high five. Turning to Josie, he held out his arm.

"Are you ready?"

Her heart sped foolishly, even as she told herself they were only sharing a couple of eggs in the most out-of-the-way restaurant she could find. One meal together and she'd head for home.

"Absolutely." Ready to battle the unwise attraction long enough to thank him for delivering her safely to shore, she dropped her fingers into the crook of his elbow.

This would be like any other friendly networking meeting, she told herself. But as her skin tingled from that small, casual touch, Josie feared her body was ready to betray her good intentions at the slightest provocation.

AN HOUR OF BREAKING BREAD with Josie had yielded a wealth of useful information about her. They hadn't found a restaurant still serving breakfast at noon, so they'd settled for sandwiches and microbrews at a quiet local pub.

Now, while they finished off the last of the beer and waited for the check, Keith steered the conversation back to his discovery that she was as much a workaholic as he'd been up until this week. Apparently, she'd worked in the fashion industry after college, then taken a job at a large interior-decorating firm before starting her own company eighteen months ago.

"So, you know, I'm taking a vacation for the first time in three years." He kept his empty longneck in his hand, hoping the waitress would be slow to return, since he still wanted to learn more about the woman across from him in the tall, private booth. "When's the last time you took a stab at some rest and relaxation?"

"Hmm." She played with the unused knife near her plate, flipping the heavy piece over and over on the scarred wood table. A series of skinny silver bands covered her ring finger right up to the knuckle. "I went to Mexico with some girlfriends before I started at that big interior-design firm, so that would be…two and a half years ago."

Nearby, a busboy juggled drinks for a corner table full of older women who'd ordered a big, candle-covered birthday cake a little while ago.

"Almost as long as me." Keith shifted in his seat, his knee lightly grazing hers. Once. Twice. Until she looked up at him, almost as if to accuse him of flirting with her on purpose. But his expression must have remained neutral enough, because she went back to playing with her knife.

Her cheeks had gone warm again, though, and he noticed she soon set aside the knife to take a drink of her water. He was determined not to let this attraction get the better of him today, determined to pursue her without getting lost in her dark eyes.

"Yes. I think I'm overdue for a vacation." Her lips were damp from the water glass, shiny and kissable. "But I'm really trying to lock down a shot at a cable show to bring local decorating inspiration to people in the Boston market."

With an effort, he pulled his attention away from her lips while a group at the bar broke out in raucous laughter. The establishment wasn't packed to capacity, but it was plenty busy for the midday meal.

"Which means you have no intention of taking a vacation anytime soon." Keith had made enough excuses to friends over the years that he recognized the blow-off. The certainty that it was better to work than to play.

No doubt about it, Josie was driven.

"Well, I hired an employee a few months ago, so if I fail now, it's not just me who loses out on a paycheck. Plus—" she released the knife and rested her fingers on the table, not all that far from his "—I'm trying to get out from under college loans and some financial help my parents gave me when I was starting out. I've come to the point where I don't want to feel I owe anyone anything."

He wanted to move her plate aside and cover her hand with his. Stroke each finger and plant a kiss in the middle of her palm before venturing up her arm. He remembered exactly how smooth she felt from those brief touches the night before.

"That's admirable." Keith tried to keep the thread of the conversation, knowing he had to be on his game if he hoped to convince her to take a chance with him. "It's rewarding to build a company from the ground up. It took a lot of effort to get Green Principles off the ground, but it was really worth it."

The deal he had brewing now, in fact, would make them a global affiliate with the Wholesome Branding marketing firm. Green Principles services would be automatically offered and recommended to all Wholesome Branding clients. Keith's company was entering a new phase of growth.

"So what does your firm do, exactly?" She'd asked attentive business questions all through lunch, keeping the conversation on less personal footing wherever possible. Which made it damn difficult to proposition her.

He kept wondering if she remembered much of what he'd said to her the night before. Did she recall him touching her? He clenched his fingers, fighting the need to remind her.

"We're a consulting company." He focused on the words and wished he hadn't finished his drink. "We hire out to big business to help them navigate increasingly tough environmental laws and to create environmental initiatives unique to their industry. Our goal is to help them be more than just compliant, but actually cutting edge."

The company had started out so high-minded and grassroots oriented that he'd been surprised by how lucrative the business had become. Astonishing how much a guy could accomplish when he focused on work instead of finding the right woman. Of course, that meant he hadn't had a date in a dog's age....

And, amazingly, Josie appeared interested. Not just in him, but in his work, too.

"Hey, folks." Their flustered waitress, with a ketchup

stain on her blouse and a trayful of empty glasses, paused at the table. "Sorry to take so long, but we're short a busboy today." After sliding the bill across the table, she removed their plates. "I hear we've got a cold front coming our way. No rain yet, I hope."

Josie peered between the beer signs in the window toward the street. "It was nice out when we came in," she replied, reaching for the slip of paper.

Over his dead body.

"No way." He snatched the check with ease, the appropriate bill already in his hand. He put them both on the waitress's tray alongside the empty glasses. "I'm buying your silence with this meal, remember?"

While the waitress helped his cause, hurrying away amid protests, Keith realized their time together was drawing short and he hadn't accomplished nearly enough over lunch to justify propositioning Josie quite yet. Damn it.

They left the pub and walked out into the midday sunlight. He steered her toward a wooden bench by the sidewalk to discuss where to go next. The downtown area remained quiet now that the high tourist season had come to a close. But a few rented mopeds and bicycles filled a rack nearby. He didn't want Josie to leave, but convincing a woman he'd known for less than twenty-four hours to get back on board the *Vesta* with him to sail off into the unknown was unlikely.

Working against him was most of what he'd learned over lunch—that her ambition rivaled his own, that she never took time off and that she would be "thrilled" to make a pitch to Murphy Resorts should they ever be interested in exploring design alternatives at any of their properties. In fact, as a man who'd been hit on by business prospects of his own in the past, he'd recognized Josie's smooth redirecting of the conversation anytime he'd veered into mildly flirtatious terrain.

But he'd learned something else intriguing about her over lunch.

She wanted him.

That wasn't arrogance on his part. It was fact. It didn't matter that she presented a charming professional image. He could tell by the way her pupils widened when he leaned closer that she wasn't as unaffected as she pretended. Then there'd been moments when her gaze had lingered on him those extra few seconds before she looked away, her cheeks turning a shade of pink that didn't come from a makeup compact.

The signs were there. It was just a matter of helping her act on it.

"So what's your time frame for the trip to Charleston?" she asked, hovering by the bench he'd pointed out, then peering back to a storefront behind them. "Actually, before you answer that, would you mind terribly if we popped into this store for a clean shirt so I can return the one I borrowed?"

She plucked at the worn cotton fabric of his brother's too-large tee that said Navy in big block letters. On Josie, it read Av, since the other letters were hidden in the excess material at her sides.

"Sure." He regretted not thinking of it himself. He'd

been so focused on getting what he wanted with her, he'd neglected to consider what she needed. An oversight he would not repeat. As they approached the boutique, he held the door for her. "I'll be curious to see if a decorator spends a lot of time choosing clothes or if the professional eye makes the process faster."

She slid past him into the dim, artsy store filled with more mannequins than actual clothes, her slight figure barely stirring a breeze, yet commanding attention even in an oversize T-shirt. Something about the way she carried herself—confident and brisk—gave the impression she was someone important, someone people should recognize.

After greeting the salesclerk with a wave, Josie peered back at Keith over her shoulder.

"Normally, I dress with the same care I'd use when decorating a room, since the way I look is kind of an advertisement for the business." She moved toward a rack full of white blouses, and walked her fingers through the hangers in search of the right size. "I mean, who would trust a decorator who shows up in yoga pants and a T-shirt? Clients expect someone in my line of work to look more put together."

Moving through the store with efficiency, she had two shirts and a pair of pants in hand already. As she turned toward the next rack, he anticipated the move and stepped in front of her. Surprising her. Surprising himself, to a certain extent. He hadn't planned to make his play for her here and now, but he didn't want to wait any longer.

The dimly lit, overly air-conditioned store created an odd sense of privacy, since the loud, pulsing music isolated them from the lone salesclerk chatting away on a cell phone at the counter in the back of the shop.

"I hope you don't see me as a client you need to impress." He calculated their distance in inches. Not nearly close enough. Still, her elbow brushed his chest as she clutched the hangers to her.

Belatedly, she retracted her arm, tightening her grip on the clothes as if she could halt the attraction between them by not touching him. He hoped like hell that trick wouldn't work.

"I know better than to presume anyone will sign on with me," she protested, carefully keeping things on a safe footing. "You haven't even seen my work—"

Waving off her words, he shook his head.

"Not because of that. I'm sure you're very good at what you do. What I meant was, I hope you won't let business get in the way of something…better." He had to put his cards on the table soon or she'd be dressed in new clothes and penciling him into her appointment book for a sales pitch before they said goodbye.

"Hey, hon," the young salesclerk shouted to Josie over the loud music, one hand over her cell phone to muffle her voice. "The fitting room is in the back. There's a place where your friend can have a seat while you try stuff on."

She gestured toward an archway near a shoe rack, the huge cocktail ring she wore glinting under one of the store's blue spotlights.

And thank you, Miss Disinterested Salesgirl. She'd just given Keith the break he'd been looking for.

"Can we talk for a minute?" He took the clothes from Josie's arms. "Let me carry these for you."

Judging from her expression, she had mixed feelings about a conversation in the dressing room. But hey, if he was going to give her a hard sell on the merits of spending more time with him, better to do it in a public place where she knew she could walk away, than on the boat, where she might feel trapped.

He led her under the arch near the shoe rack. A love seat had been situated near a small table holding a coffeepot and a pitcher of water. The sofa sat across from a three-way mirror. A smaller room with a bench inside was visible beyond a half-drawn velvet curtain.

Behind him, Josie's flat shoes clicked double-time to keep up. He used his lead to deposit the clothes she'd chosen in the fitting area, then he backed away to sit on an arm of the love seat so he didn't look like some loser in the market to catch a view of her naked. Not that he wasn't in the market, per se. But he had every intention of waiting until she offered that opportunity to him freely.

"I'm not sure—" she began.

He rushed to cut off that line of thinking.

"I'll get out of your way in a minute," he assured her, vaguely wondering why he felt so compelled to push her for more. "But I want you to do me a favor and think about something first."

In his mind, he had a game plan. He'd list the reasons

she needed a vacation and why he was in the ideal position to give her that break right now. He would admit his attraction and dare her to deny her own.

Right now, though, she stood close enough to touch. Her sexy brown eyes tracked his every movement as he stepped even closer. No one could see them. In the distance, the salesclerk gabbed on as if she wanted the world to hear about her weekend plans with a guy her father hated. And the electric chime on the front door would alert them when anyone else came into the store.

Keith's game plan shifted in a hurry.

"Something for your consideration…" He bracketed her shoulders in his palms. Steadying her.

Right before he gambled everything on a kiss.

4

JOSIE'S HEART FLUTTERED wildly. Palms damp, knees shaky, she had all she could do to stay still as Keith leaned closer. More than anything, she wanted to meet him halfway. Or maybe tackle him in the fitting room and pull the curtain so no one could see.

But no, every bit of restraint she could muster amounted to her waiting like a deer in the headlights for her tall, sexy sea captain to lay claim to her mouth just the way she'd dreamed the night before. When the soft warmth of his lips brushed hers—once, twice, with slow deliberation—she thought she'd melt on contact. Sweet sensation flooded her veins and sent an undeniable bolt of heat between her thighs.

That had never happened before. Well, never so pointedly nor so quickly.

He touched only her shoulders. And, of course, her mouth. The rest of her swayed toward him like a magnet, the draw of anticipation too powerful to resist. The music blaring over the store's speakers—an angsty punk-rock ballad—seared into her brain, forever associated with the man and the moment. Like a love scene swelling to crescendo on-screen in time with the gut-wrenching lyrics, Josie wrapped her arms around his neck and hauled him closer, pressing herself to him.

She couldn't recall any reason why she shouldn't be with this man. Right now, she could only think about how much she wanted this. Him.

He speared a hand through the hair at the back of her head, anchoring her. His other palm spanned her lower back, his pinkie straying onto the curve of her hip, stirring the low, liquid heat.

"Come with me," he urged, the request surprisingly possible given the way her body was responding.

"Not here," she murmured, her overeager imagination trying to think of a better alternative. "Somewhere private…"

He edged back the barest fraction, his green eyes finding hers in the dim, moody lighting of the store.

"I meant—" He closed his eyes for a moment and she had the feeling he was trying to get a grip on himself.

In fact, she'd almost bet on that, since the rigid length of his arousal nudged her belly.

Before she could apologize for plastering herself to him like silk with a static-cling problem, he opened his eyes again and took a deep breath.

"Josie, I want you to come with me on this trip to Charleston. It's my first vacation in forever and it could be yours, too. I'm not sure how long it will take—a week or more, depending on the weather." He sucked in another deep breath, and it seemed to her he was willing his whole body back under control. "We could explore this thing between us...."

A wicked impulse made her roll her hips against him.

"I'd love to check it out thoroughly," she admitted, scarcely able to believe he was propositioning such a thing, let alone that she would even joke about taking off with him on a sexcapade thinly disguised as a shared vacation.

"I mean it." He lifted his palm to her cheek and the gesture felt so...familiar.

She wanted to close her eyes and absorb the feel of him. To listen to him talk to her.

"I can't just leave town for a week," she protested, though her eyelids fluttered.

She could hear footsteps on the hardwood floor, and they were coming this way. She edged back from Keith just in time to see the waif-thin salesclerk turn the corner into the dressing area.

"Anything I can get for you folks?" the clerk asked, her eyes taking a slow path up and down Keith's powerfully male physique.

"Not yet, but I'm working on a list," Keith replied, never taking his eyes off Josie, his palm still cradling her cheek.

"Sure thing," the young woman agreed, licking thoroughly painted lips while she stared her fill.

Not that Josie could blame her. She found it a challenge to look away, too.

But honestly, she couldn't spend her afternoon salivating over a handsome man. With regret she stepped back from him as the clerk finally departed. Keith's hands returned to his sides while her every nerve ending protested his absence.

"I'm sorry." She really was. A fling with an extremely desirable man would be more than welcome right now. "But I need to get back to Chatham to meet with Chase and nail down that contract. Plus, I have other projects to follow up on in Boston if I want to keep meeting my payroll. I can't afford a vacation."

"Okay." Keith retreated to the love seat. He sat forward, elbows on his knees, his fingers propped in a steeple. "But will you humor me while we look at this from another angle?"

He waved toward the dressing room and she took the opportunity to try on her clothes.

"It won't help," she warned him, stepping behind the heavy velvet curtain and drawing it shut. "But I'll listen while I change."

Quickly, she tugged off the big tee he'd given her and wriggled out of her jeans, her skin overheated and sensitive.

"Let's say for a moment that money wasn't an object." His deep voice carried over the curtain rod, over her. Then the words sank in.

She tensed, hearing the breezy, entitled voices of her parents in those words.

"Money is always an object," she countered, refusing to embody the media's definition of her as a trust-fund baby.

She'd worked too hard for her independence, and wouldn't give it up now.

"I agree. But let's assume we can find a practical way to work around that problem for now. Do you have any other objections to this proposition? For example, do you feel I'm jumping the gun on this?"

Something about his forthright confrontation of the issue pleased her. The tension in her shoulders relaxed as she tugged the khaki capri pants off the hanger.

"Not really." Maybe that would be the quickest way to shut down this insane conversation, but she didn't feel right lying to him after he'd been so direct with her, so thoughtful and charming. "You were kind enough to call the Coast Guard for me last night. And you brought me into shore first thing today. That was really considerate, when you could have just cashed in on an attraction I probably didn't hide very well."

The moment of silence made her wonder what he was thinking.

"Keith?" What if someone else had entered the dressing area out there while she babbled away about ridiculously private things?

"I'm here." There was a rich, smoky note in his voice again that made her shiver as she slid into the blouse. "I was just thinking about the way you responded to me last night while you were sleeping."

"I knew something happened!" she accused, tugging aside the curtain far enough to glare at him.

Until his hot gaze reminded her her blouse wasn't

buttoned. She wrenched the velvet barrier closed again, her pulse thrumming hard.

"All I did was talk to you." His voice loomed closer.

She swallowed, her mouth gone dry.

"So what did you say?" She believed him, trusting her instinct that he would not take advantage of a sleeping woman. He could have had half her clothes off during that kiss earlier, but he'd been admirably restrained.

Besides, she was so strangely turned on by his voice, it made total sense that he might have said things to her in her sleep.

"I told you what I wanted to do to you," he admitted, the rich, male timbre mere inches from her ear on the other side of the velvet drape.

She swore she could feel the warmth of his body through the curtain. Beneath the cups of her bra, her breasts beaded. Her fingers twined around the fabric of her unbuttoned blouse to keep from reaching out to touch him.

"Like what?" she prodded, needing to know. Wondering if his suggestive words had inspired the dreams she'd had all night.

"I suggested I remove your clothes with my teeth."

Her breath hitched. No, she forgot how to breathe altogether.

"I dreamed about that." In vivid detail. "Among other things."

"Will you let me in?" He must have tapped the curtain because the fabric billowed gently. "Just for a minute?"

That would be dangerous. But she'd never felt so turned on by a man with so little prompting. The chemistry that simmered between them wasn't your everyday garden variety of male-female interest. It was like a biological necessity imprinted on her DNA, urging her toward him.

"Yes." She had the feeling it would be the first of more affirmatives she would whisper for this man.

And then he was in the dressing room with her, behind the velvet curtain and isolated from anyone else in the store. The spotlight overhead burnished his dark hair with a blue glow. His green eyes set fire to her skin as they roamed over her half-dressed body. But all she could think about was his teeth going to work on the straps and buttons that remained, peeling away everything she wore until she was utterly naked, vulnerable to him.

"You liked it when I talked to you, Josie." His voice rumbled in her ear, soft and warm, for her alone.

She closed the distance between them, pressing herself to him again, once more initiating the contact that he withheld. Out of noble intent? Or to see how far she would go?

"How did you know?" She kissed his jaw, inhaling the dark spice of his aftershave. "How could you tell I liked it if I was sleeping?"

His cheek shifted beneath her lips and she could tell he was smiling.

"You made these sexy sounds. Little humming noises. And when I stopped, you arched toward me like you wanted more."

"Wicked man," she chastised, even as she stepped between his thighs.

The picture they made in the dressing room mirror was almost more than she could bear without throwing herself at him and wrapping her legs around his waist. His body looked all the more powerful next to her petite frame. His strong calves and taut butt promised pleasure for as long as she wanted what he could give her....

"Sir?" The feminine trill of the young salesclerk came through the curtain, a smirk evident in the only word she spoke.

"Yes?" Keith's voice was curt, but his gaze remained warm all over Josie's body.

"I put together the things you requested and I got an overnight bag from the shop next door. You're all set." The woman sounded so breathless Josie wondered how far she'd had to run for that overnight bag.

And what, exactly, had Keith ordered from a women's apparel shop? Pulling her thoughts back to reality, Josie stepped away from him and buttoned the blouse. She'd buy it and wear it out of the store, preferably the sooner the better, since lingering with him only tempted her sorely.

"Thank you," he returned. "We're almost done."

"No hurry." The clerk gave a girlish giggle as her steps faded away.

"What did you buy?" Josie queried, leaving the

khakis in place, too, since she knew it would be a mistake to undress in front of him.

Her skin was already way too oversensitive, her body completely susceptible to him. If she ever took her pants off around him, she knew exactly what would happen next.

"I thought it prudent to plan for all eventualities." He handed her the purse she'd dropped on the floor earlier, giving every appearance of affording her some space.

But by now she had his number.

"You bought clothes for me, didn't you?" She needed to be careful around a man who could appear so accommodating while skillfully maneuvering to what he wanted. "You went ahead and purchased things for a trip I can't possibly take."

"When faced with impossible odds, I think it's best to eliminate the obstacles, one by one. Your lack of attire is an obstacle that's now been removed." He said it so seriously, so earnestly, she couldn't help but laugh.

"Wow." She shook her head as she settled her purse strap on one shoulder, preparing to leave the dressing room and put some distance between her and this man. "I'll bet you're a force to be reckoned with at the bargaining table."

"Try me." He spread his hands as if to say *bring it on.* "Why not test the strength of my negotiating skills and tell me what else is holding you back from going with me?"

Something about his complete confidence in himself made her want to play devil's advocate.

"What if I said I'm just not that into you?"

He didn't hesitate.

"I'd kiss you again and see if you were still singing the same tune five minutes from now."

And...yeah. No sense tempting fate. She remembered the effect his kiss had on her. The bell chiming at the entrance door to the store called her back from pleasant memories of Keith's mouth on hers.

She needed to finish this conversation and return to Boston before she tossed her good sense aside and sailed off into the sunset with a stranger.

"Assuming you're correct about that..." Her voice scratched on a dry note and she had to clear her throat. "Then my hesitation comes down to two things. One is a financial necessity for me to keep working. The other is more complicated, and I'd rather not delve into those waters, since the economics alone are reason enough. Okay?"

"You can redecorate Jack's boat," he suggested, undeterred. "It'll be my Christmas present to him and his soon-to-be fiancée to take the *Vesta* from vintage bachelor pad to something more family oriented." He kept his voice low, now that they could hear other customers in the store. The music muffled the words, but they could still hear the patter of conversation and laughter on the sales floor.

"No." Josie was shaking her head before he finished. "That makes sex a business transaction, and I wouldn't take a job from you if we went on this trip together. But—strictly out of curiosity—I thought you were selling this boat for Jack and bringing it to the buyer in Charleston?"

Wasn't that the whole purpose of his voyage?

"He thinks I am. I mean, that's what I agreed to do. But I have reason to believe he's going to get back together with his ex-girlfriend this week, and, since the boat was an important part of their relationship, I think he's going to change his mind about selling the *Vesta*."

"So conceivably, we wouldn't even go all the way to Charleston?" She had no idea how he could intuit a reunion between his brother and an ex, but she was beginning to realize Keith Murphy wasn't the kind of man you doubted. "Not that I'm seriously considering the trip."

But if it was only a couple of days, to take the edge off this hungry, restless feeling, maybe the trip wasn't as impossible as she'd thought. And who would see them together in the middle of the Atlantic? It wasn't as if they'd resurrect the old scandal, when no one knew they were together.

"Probably not. But I can't stay near Chatham or it could jeopardize the reunion between those two." Briefly, he explained how he'd made a bet with his brother to swap boats, knowing Jack's ex would be on the other one. "I can't make it too easy for him to weasel out of the wager and take his own boat back. Those two need some time together to work things out."

"You're matchmaking." She found that…adorable. There was no better word.

And knowing he harbored a tender side beneath his arrogance attracted her all the more.

Keith scowled. "I'm shoving the jackass in the right direction. Call it what you will." Tugging open the curtain to the dressing room, he held it aside but didn't step out yet. "So how about we agree to just a couple of days headed south? I'll stick close to the shore and we can navigate inland on Wednesday morning. You can check on your business and return to Boston if you want."

She recognized that he was making it easy for her to leave. The choice remained hers alone.

Damn, but it was a gamble. She hadn't even mentioned her other fear. She couldn't bear for the party-girl image to return. The accusation that she'd been as hedonistic as her parents had cut deep, especially given how hard she'd tried to forge a path away from their wealthy lifestyle.

She'd learned her lesson, and was now more conservative in how she promoted her business, avoiding the nightclub scene and the movers and shakers who lived on the society pages.

Yet Keith Murphy's family was a staple in the Boston media. If word got out about her spending time sailing the Eastern Seaboard with Keith, she'd be right back to being depicted as the spoiled, pampered offspring of obscenely rich parents.

But they sure weren't in Boston now. And it had been far too long since she'd indulged in the kind of fun this man promised. Hadn't Marlena been after her to take a couple days off? Maybe she would return to work as recharged as her assistant suggested.

"Okay," she agreed, before she had a chance to talk herself out of it. "If we can head inland on Wednesday, I could afford to take a couple of days to relax."

The white-hot flame that flared in Keith's eyes suggested relaxation wasn't his primary concern. And just like that, her temperature spiked in answer.

"I've got a few ideas to help you unwind," he assured her, his arm sliding around her waist as he guided her toward the door. "And the sooner we get started the better."

HIS BUSINESS SKILLS came in handy for organizing a trip with Josie. On the way back to the *Vesta,* Keith encouraged her to pick up any personal necessities while he arranged for the clothes he'd bought to be delivered to the south wharf, where they'd docked. He called in an order to a local gourmet shop to stock their fridge with a few specialty items and enough food for a week. Another phone call took care of purchasing new sheets and extra towels, also to be delivered. Finally, he touched base with the marina's housekeeping service to spruce up the boat and ensure all the delivery people were quickly accommodated.

As the afternoon grew warmer and the streets crowded with day-trippers who'd taken the ferry over for an outing, Keith celebrated his victory in negotiating a couple days with Josie.

He still couldn't believe she'd said yes.

That lone affirmative marked his biggest coup yet. He couldn't wait to have her all to himself. Even now, as he waited outside the cedar-sided pharmacy where she'd disappeared to buy shampoo, he had to fight the urge to haul her back to the boat, where they could lock a door behind them.

Their time alone in the dressing room had been sweetly torturous. His kiss proved to Josie the chemistry was there, but it had taken a toll on him, too. His whole body was so primed for her, he'd had to exercise all his will to harness the hunger during their last-minute preparations.

To distract himself while he waited, he checked his email, tying up some loose ends at the office. He leaned against a tree trunk as a jogger ran past with three little dogs on leashes. Two women, clutching iced coffees and too many packages, dropped onto the bench near him as he set up his email's auto-respond feature to forward an associate's contact information. Then he double-checked the weather report, before sending an email to the owner of Wholesome Branding, the marketing firm interested in offering Green Principles services to all their clients.

Keith kept his tone light, mentioning his plan to head south for a few days in case their paths could cross during this trip. The head honcho at Wholesome was surprisingly reclusive for a marketing guy, but his home base was on the Virginia coast, so maybe this trip would provide a chance for them to outline parameters for a partnership.

But right now, Keith's main goal was Josie. Just thinking about her sent an electric jolt over his skin. No, wait. That sensation derived from the fact that she was walking toward him, a small package from the pharmacy in one hand and a canvas shopping bag in the other. She'd pulled her hair back in a ponytail and a new blue-and-white-striped ribbon held it in place on one shoulder. Big sunglasses hid most of her face, like a movie star trying hard to stay incognito.

She carried herself with the grace of a dancer, her petite frame sliding easily through the crowd of late-day shoppers. But her neat presence and hesitant smile hid a sultry side. He'd seen hints of her hidden sensuality the night before, when she'd given that throaty moan in response to his seductive words. And today, in the dressing room... There was no telling what might have happened if that salesclerk hadn't called through the curtain when she did.

Signing out of his online account, Keith jammed his PDA in his pocket and met Josie on the sidewalk, taking her bags. He drew her aside to make room for a group of schoolkids ambling down the street in matching yellow T-shirts behind their leader, who wore a three-cornered hat and narrated the outing.

"Are you ready?" Keith figured the boat ought to be well stocked by now. He'd paid enough to ensure timely service.

To ensure he didn't have to wait much longer to touch this woman.

"I think so." She glanced down at the packages she'd

handed him and then nodded, her cheeks flushing that shade of pink that drove him crazy. "Yes."

He wouldn't call it a full-on blush, but a tinge of color that hinted at the same keen awareness he felt. He couldn't wait to uncover every possibility for inciting that reaction.

Soon, he'd put his lips on her cheek to test if he could feel the warmth there or just see it. For that matter, he planned to put his mouth all over Josie Passano before the sun set, just as soon as they'd sailed far enough from Nantucket to be sure they were well and truly alone. While he'd made practical plans for their voyage together, they didn't come close to the level of strategy he would deploy in uncovering ways to pleasure the woman next to him.

And thanks to her telling reactions to his erotic suggestions last night, he knew exactly where to begin.

5

IT DIDN'T MATTER that Josie made intelligent, pleasant conversation with Keith the whole way back to the sailboat. It also didn't matter that she was genuinely intrigued by his business, an innovative company that made her want to investigate more green options for decorating.

Because just under the respectable, ladylike surface, thoughts of sex seethed inside her.

Who knew she harbored such deep, earthy hungers?

Once Keith had the *Vesta* speeding into the wind, Josie tipped her face toward the light sea spray kicked up from the water, to cool off her skin. Actually, they were sideways to the wind, she thought. While she'd been watching him move around the boat to prepare it for sailing, Keith had talked her through the physics of how to set the sheets to maximize speed. She remembered something about not traveling directly downwind, but having the breeze come from an angle—though, admittedly, she had been mostly thinking about how soon she would taste his mouth on hers again.

"This is wonderful," she observed, holding her arms up to feel the breeze through her fingers. "It's like I'm airing out my mind."

Her ponytail, and the ribbon she'd tied around it, blew against her neck. She felt freer out on the water with no need to worry about anyone spotting them together. It wasn't as if she and Keith were celebrities. But in Nantucket she'd been nervous that he might see someone he knew, and the rumor mill would start churning. On the open water, all alone, those worries melted away.

"Have you sailed before?" he asked, his white shirt stretching along his shoulders as he tugged on a line to tighten one of the sheets—a jib, maybe? She hoped there wouldn't be a quiz on all the things he'd showed her. She could secure beams and lines just fine as long as he pointed her in the right direction.

"A few times with my parents when I was very young," she admitted. "But they were usually too busy mixing cocktails on the deck to pay any attention to how the crew operated the boat."

Securing the line in its new position, Keith looked her way and grinned. "Then it's a good thing they hired someone else to captain the vessel."

"I guess." She'd grown so accustomed to seeing the darker side of her upbringing that she'd gotten out of the habit of justifying her parents' decisions. "But I would have enjoyed learning the ropes instead of worrying about one of them going overboard."

Sunlight slanted across the water, a fiery trail of wavering orange. Beside them, the ocean surface had smoothed until the hull chased one lone wave as it cut through the sea. For a moment, Josie worried she'd revealed too much, spoiled the unspoken pact that a two-day fling meant keeping things light and simple between them.

But Keith's gaze traveled the main mast, his faraway expression suggesting he hadn't noticed.

"My father made certain we could all sail—me and my four brothers. Later, when our foster brother came to live with us, we taught him, too."

"I'm sure that was wise, since you grew up on the water."

His eyes turned back to her, questioning.

"I saw pictures of your house in a decorating magazine once," she explained. "I remember it's perched on a hill overlooking the ocean. I know if I had kids in a house like that, I'd want to be sure they could swim and operate a boat safely."

"I'm not sure safety was Robert Murphy's number-one concern." Keith shook his head. "The point was to make us as competitive as possible."

"He must have spent a lot of time with you." Peering up at the broad white sheets snapping in the breeze, she admired the simple beauty of the boat. "Sailing takes a while to master."

Leaving his sails and his lines, Keith sauntered

toward her, his polo shirt plastered to his body, over the white tee underneath. Josie wanted to wrestle both garments off him and absorb the texture of his skin with her palms. She could anticipate the response of all that hard muscle at her fingertips, and she liked the vision her imagination supplied.

"He did." Her dark-haired Adonis paused mere inches from her, close enough for her to feel the heat of his body close to hers. "And I suppose that should count for something."

"It's flattering when someone wants to spend time with you," she observed lightly. Not even thoughts of her parents' lack of interest in her could distract her from the desire to drag Keith down to the built-in seat on the aft deck.

No one would see them if a boat happened by and they were lying down.

"Hell, yes, it's flattering." He tipped her chin up so their gazes met, and she realized she'd been staring at the seat cushions. "And wouldn't I love to know where your thoughts go when you get this color in your cheeks."

Her fingers flew to her face, where she could sense the heat. The flush deepened with his eyes so firmly on her.

"I was just—" she glanced from the seat cushions to him "—wondering how long you were going to be busy with your captain duties."

He scanned the horizon quickly, something she noticed he did often while the boat was under way.

"There's a warm front brewing behind us and a cold front to the south, which means storms could develop. We want to keep an eye out for any changes in the weather, but until then, we should take advantage of the wind. Besides, I didn't think it was right to tell you I'd take you on a trip and then use it as an excuse just to get you aboard. Alone." The rich rumble of his voice sent a shiver of pleasure through her.

"Then how about this?" She closed the gap between them, her fingers alighting on his chest to explore the broad expanse of muscle there. "I told you I would take this trip as an excuse to get *you* on board. Away from the rest of the world."

She waited, knowing she didn't have the sexual assertiveness to do more than hint. Her heartbeat sped, her breathing as ragged as if she'd run an hour on the treadmill. For one long moment, Keith studied her, his green eyes turning dark as a shaded forest despite the sun casting a burnished hue over everything around them.

His hands bracketed her waist, his fingers straying onto her hips as he pulled her fully against him.

"I'm going to drop anchor in a minute," he told her, his voice a rough whisper against her ear while his hips pressed a rigid erection into her belly. "I'll find a spot to spend the night."

Wordless from the sweet sensations curling through her, she merely nodded, her cheek brushing the skin-warmed fabric of his shirt.

"Would you like that?" He moved his mouth lower,

toward her neck, pausing to gently clamp his teeth around the gold hoop in her earlobe.

"Yes," she managed to answer, tipping her head to one side to give him more access.

He nipped her ear lightly, sending another shiver through her, this one so blatant it might have been embarrassing if she wasn't so completely turned on.

His teeth, she realized, as he placed a kiss on the column of her throat. That's what had her all breathless and hungry inside. He'd made her think about him undressing her again.

"In fact," she added, her voice hoarse with restrained passion, "the sooner you can put the brakes on this thing, the sooner you'll see the surprise I've got in store for you downstairs."

"You're incentive enough." He cupped his hands on her hips, squeezing gently. "Although I'm curious now."

"I'll give you a hint." She extricated herself from his arms in the hopes of enticing him below deck as soon as possible. "It's teeth-friendly."

AN HOUR FELT LIKE three days.

Keith raced through the process of securing the *Vesta,* taking the extra time to steer toward an outcropping of rocks that could hardly be called an island, just so he'd have a shallow place to set the anchor. Yet every minute he spent preparing the boat for the night felt interminable when he knew Josie was close by, waiting for him.

His head ached, possibly from grinding his teeth for

the last hour, the delay turning downright painful. He couldn't remember ever wanting a woman like this. To distract himself, he thought briefly about their conversation earlier, when she'd rerouted the talk from family to the attraction between them. The way she'd admired his father's investment in his kids made Keith think that one or both of her parents hadn't made much of an investment in her. Just a hunch, but he was pretty good at reading people.

Obviously, Josie didn't want to spend time talking about her family. And while he was curious about her background, he had no reason to press. Right now, he just wanted to be with her.

Finally, he flipped on the lights to ensure they would be visible to oncoming vessels even after the sun set—which would happen momentarily. With the sails furled and the lines tied, Keith shut off everything else except the radio.

It took an effort not to sprint across the deck and leap down the companionway like a freaking superhero. But somehow he managed to restrain himself to a jog—past the aft deck seating, down the few stairs that led to the galley and main salon, where he'd first discovered her the night before.

Where she'd taken up residence once again.

"Hello, Keith." Josie's throaty greeting drifted from inside a ring of candles.

Golden light flickered warmly, transforming the utilitarian boat interior into something out of a dream. Josie sat at the center, her silky dark hair falling to the shoulders of an equally dark robe, the shimmering liquid fabric of which pooled around her. Rising, she took a step toward him, and he realized she was taller than usual.

Platform heels with elaborate straps covered her feet.

"I think I'm underdressed for whatever you've got in mind." He couldn't take his eyes off her, knowing she'd gone to all this trouble for him. The clothes. The candles.

"On the contrary, you've been overdressed virtually every time I've seen you." A wicked gleam in her eye reminded him that beneath this glamorous exterior lurked an earthy, sensual woman.

"You think?" He scrubbed a hand over his chest, where his unbuttoned polo shirt met his T-shirt.

"I *know*." She reached for the hem of the polo, all business. "But I'm going to fix that problem for you now."

Her fingers skimmed up his abs, the fabric bunching in her hands as she gathered it. He lifted his arms, helping her pull the shirt up and off.

"Nice." She ran her palms over the T-shirt, where the outline of his every muscle was obvious. "Very nice."

Peering up at him in the candlelight, she looked like some otherworldly goddess with her ankle-length silk robe and her pale, perfect skin. He wasn't a man given to fanciful thinking. But she was a walking, talking fantasy.

"Thank you." He slid one knuckle over her cheek, absorbing the smooth feel of her skin, amazed he'd lucked into meeting her at all.

She lowered her head to place a kiss on his chest. "No need to thank me. It's not a compliment. It's a fact."

His skin twitched where her lips had been. The need to get naked with her was a flame licking through him.

"No. I meant I'm grateful that you're here. For this." He gestured toward the candles.

"Don't thank me yet. You haven't even seen your surprise." Her hand went to the robe tie.

He held his breath.

At a deft flick of her fingers, the ribbon at her waist fell away. The lapels of the robe drifted apart. And the outfit that came into view robbed him of speech.

Draped in silver sequins, she wore some kind of costume that would have suited a burlesque queen. Meant to tantalize without revealing too much, the metallic bustier glittered as she moved, her breasts thrust upward so high it seemed an architectural feat that the fabric hid her nipples. Rhinestone straps on her shoulders held the garment in place, each tiny gem winking at him in the candlelight as she pushed the robe the rest of the way off.

Speechless, he could only gaze in amazement at the way the fabric hugged her waist and turned into silver lace around her hips. Barely there lace panties met the hem of the corset, but were trapped behind more glittery straps that held transparent stockings in place.

"I know it's not the usual boating attire, but sometimes it's tough to ignore my penchant for decorating." She spoke in a rush, possibly battling a moment's unease, since he hadn't managed to unglue his tongue from the roof of his mouth to say anything yet.

He swallowed hard. Licked his lips.

"It's fantastic." He didn't just want her. He was damn well humbled that she'd gone to so much effort for him. "Will you stay here for just a second?"

She nodded, her dark hair sliding along that pale skin, covering some of the rhinestones on those tantalizing straps.

He brushed past her and charged through the galley to the berth, where a queen-size bed had been made up neatly with new sheets by the cleaning service. Bypassing that, he yanked out a trundle from underneath and wrestled its smaller mattress through the door, back out into the main salon, where Josie waited.

"Oh!" She hurried to move a few candles, probably because, trailing blankets as he was, he posed a fire hazard. "Let me help."

Distracted by the jiggle of mouthwatering breasts as she came close, he would have probably torched the whole boat if she hadn't been there to steer him into the middle of the space.

"I want you to stay right here, in the center of all the candles," he explained belatedly, knowing his brain wasn't communicating well with his mouth. "You look so damn incredible."

He tossed the mattress on the floor near the built-in table, then dragged the fallen blankets closer.

"Want to know the best part?" She edged closer, her

sky-high heel brushing his calf as he knelt to arrange the bedding.

His gaze moved to her legs. "It's going to be tough to name any one best part." He hooked a hand around her ankle and skimmed it up the back of her silk stocking, pausing at the soft hollow behind her knee.

He watched her expression shift, her eyelids fluttering at the touch.

"No. I meant—" She gasped as he leaned near to plant a kiss on the side of her thigh, just above where he touched her.

Beneath the finely spun threads of her stocking, he could feel her skin against his lips. The scent of her was sweet and fragrant.

"Tea rose," he guessed, peering up the gorgeous length of her body to her face.

"You know your perfumes," she murmured, tangling her fingers in his hair.

"Actually, I know my teas. Green Principles consults with a tea company and they send me cool stuff every Christmas. The rose tea smells the best." He parted his lips for another kiss, licking that same small patch of her skin. "Tastes good, too."

The sound Josie made in the back of her throat was a turn-on unlike any other.

The need to possess her flared hot, and he palmed the backs of her thighs to draw her closer. His heart slammed hard against his chest, his whole body poised and throbbing with a hunger damn near all-consuming.

"You said something about this outfit being teeth-friendly." He nipped the satin bow that rested over one garter clasp. "Did you mean these?"

Not waiting for an answer, he hooked his teeth around the tab and raised it enough to slide free of the slot, loosening the strap's hold on the silvery silk encasing her thigh. He covered the newly bared skin with his mouth, drawing on her gently until she half tumbled forward into him, her knees giving out in a way that sent a fierce spear of satisfaction through his chest.

"I…" She tried to steady herself with her hands on his shoulders, but he guided her down to the mattress instead. "No. That is, I meant the ribbons up the back were easy to…you know…undo."

With her pupils dilated and her breathing fast and uneven, she seemed too distracted to talk. Which was just fine with him. He'd done enough talking today, trying to convince her to take this trip with him. Now it was up to him to prove she'd made the right choice.

But if she'd gone to so much trouble to choose an outfit that would drive him out of his ever-loving mind, he wanted to at least take it in from all sides before he peeled it off her. So, curious to see the ties, he levered himself higher on the mattress to peer over her shoulder.

The black ribbon threaded through tiny eyes up the back of the corset, the whole getup held together with that fragile satin and just waiting for him to tug it free.

Trouble was, there were so many places on her that demanded his attention, he hardly knew where to begin.

She ended his dilemma by wrapping a hand around

his neck and drawing him close. Softly, she brushed her lips over his, claiming his mouth in a kiss so achingly sweet he could have blissed out on it for at least a week.

The woman was a silver flame, hotter than he could handle, sizzling him from the outside in. He palmed her spine and yanked the tie loose. The garment she wore slipped down enough that he could slide the rhinestone straps away. Free her full, sexy breasts.

He cupped them and molded them in his hands, fascinated by the upward tilt of the dark pink nipples. Lowering his mouth to first one, than the other, he laved the tight buds with hungry swipes of his tongue.

His body throbbed with the urge to be inside her, every inch of him hard and wanting. She seemed wise to that need, her hands coming to life on his abs and smoothing his T-shirt away from his shorts. Gently, she steered the zipper on his fly over his erection until he was free.

Keith felt heat searing his back as his skin—his whole being—caught fire. His hands were unsteady by the time he got around to popping the tabs on the other garter straps, enabling him to rake away the corset completely.

Naked but for the silvery panties, Josie's body was even more mind-blowing than the garment she'd been wearing. Candlelight warmed her pale skin to the color of a golden peach, the flickering glow reflected in her dark eyes as she slipped her palm inside his boxers to trail up the rigid length of him. The sensation knocked the breath out of him, holding him motionless for several long moments. Pleasure washed over him, threatening to pull him under.

He ground his teeth together, not wanting to touch her until he could again find some restraint.

"It's been too long for me," he warned, his voice sounding nothing like his own.

"Me, too." She gave a quick nod. "Hurry."

He wanted to do so much more. To tease her higher, take her places that would make her see stars. But the need to be inside her roared through him with a primal imperative he couldn't ignore.

She started to slide her fingers into the waistband of her panties, attempting to wriggle them down. He saved her the effort, yanking them off her legs and taking the stockings with them. Pitching them sideways, he paused only long enough to make sure they didn't land on a candle flame before sweeping off his boxers.

"Condom," she whispered with a raspy breath, reaching toward the table nearby. "I put them here."

"Smart thinking," he grunted, grabbing a strand of foil packets from the bench seat. "We should be well stocked since I bought a box, too."

"Great minds think alike." She ripped a square free and tore it open.

He tossed the rest aside, grateful to be done with anything requiring fine motor skills. His concentration had narrowed to this woman. The sex he'd been dying for ever since he'd stumbled across her.

With firm, steady fingers, she rolled the condom

into place. Her thigh slid between his as she began to lift herself on top of him. But he didn't have enough finesse for that right now.

In an instant, he rolled her beneath him, covering her. Bee-stung from his kisses, her lips parted when he slipped his hand between her legs and cupped her sex.

He caught her cry in a kiss, tasting her mouth while she spread her thighs wide for him. She melted over his hand like warm honey, an invitation he couldn't deny a second longer.

Hips rearing back, he positioned himself and plunged deep. Their shouts of satisfaction mingled, the sound filling the hot, steamy quarters below deck.

Satiny arms wrapped around his neck while sleek, creamy legs twined around his waist, holding him fast. Josie's breasts pressed to his chest, the full, soft weights shifting against him with each thrust of his hips. He was lost to the feel of her feminine muscles squeezing him in a slick, silken vise. Her hips arched forward to meet his each and every time, as if she needed this fulfillment just as much as he did. It seemed impossible, but he'd never felt a hunger like hers. She didn't seek pleasure passively. She rode the storm with him rising atop each wave, seeking...

He knew what. Just like they'd sparked off one another's chemistry all day, Keith understood intuitively what she needed.

Skimming a palm down her waist and over her belly, he trailed two fingers lower. Lower. When he reached the tight bundle of nerves between her legs, he circled the nub slowly. She tensed, motionless. Waiting.

On instinct, he tugged on her lower lip with his teeth, a gentle nip. All the while, he kept up the pressure on her sex. A gasp caught in her throat as the tension in her body peaked before she spasmed helplessly against him. Wave after wave of orgasmic contractions rolled through her, her slick heat squeezing him tight until he found his own pleasure. His hips went rogue on him and all he could do was hold on to Josie's shoulders while his release steamrolled through.

In the quiet aftermath, he held her against him in the candlelight, watching the shadows flicker. She lay beside him, her breath in synch with his. Their mutual fulfillment was a deep joy that would have made him feel as if he was floating even if they hadn't been on the water.

As her breathing evened out into a steady rhythm, he reached to pull one of the blankets over her. Tucking the cotton up under her chin, he was rewarded by a fleeting smile that made the shallowest of dimples in her cheek.

His chest pulled tight with a weird constriction from inside. An odd sense of tender protectiveness, maybe.

Taking a deep breath, he ignored the feeling, knowing that sex—especially great sex—could knock you for a loop. He wasn't in the market for a major relationship and neither was she.

That left him with two more days to wring every last

incredible moment out of his time with Josie before he returned her to dry land. And he didn't intend to waste it by letting messy emotions get involved.

6

Scary good.

That's what Josie would have texted in answer to Marlena's question about her time with Keith, in a message that had somehow made its way to her phone's inbox even though there was no land in sight.

Josie sat on the sailboat's foredeck in the moonlight shortly past midnight, while Keith insisted on making them a late dinner in the tiny galley kitchen below. She'd been too doped up on endorphins to argue, her whole body a languid and well-pleasured testament to Keith Murphy's talented hands. Hips. Mouth.

Yes, sex had been scary good. She tucked the phone between two cushions on the built-in bench seat while she eyed the moon overhead and inhaled the scents of basil and garlic wafting on the breeze. Her stomach rumbled in anticipation of whatever he was cooking. She might have felt guilty about falling asleep on him so quickly after the first time they'd made love, but he'd woken her up in the most delicious way, his fingers sketching light circles all over her bare skin so that she was halfway to orgasm before she even opened her eyes.

And while it was amazing and hot, and her body still soared on its own little happy cloud right now, the rational part of her sat on the *Vesta* and felt knocked off her moorings just a bit. She tugged a light fleece throw blanket over her shoulders even though she'd pulled on a pair of jeans and a T-shirt.

"I hope you're hungry."

She turned to see Keith carrying a shiny blue tray full of dishes and drinks. Hurrying to flip up a table-top surface at the end of the bench seating, she made a place for him to set it.

"Is that a boogie board?" She fingered the rope on one end of the oddly shaped tray.

Her hand bumped his as she helped him lower it, awareness still a tangible thing between them.

"If you knew my brother, you wouldn't be surprised that he stocks sports equipment over basic serving utensils." Keith turned the board a few degrees to ensure the place settings lined up with the seats on the deck. "He quit acquiring culinary skills after he learned how to toast a Pop-Tart."

"Unlike you, apparently." Her mouth watering, she reached for a napkin and laid it over her lap so she'd be ready to dig in at a moment's notice. "This smells amazing."

"Polenta pasticciata—polenta with tomato sauce and

cheese." He poured water from a pitcher for both of them and tossed a lime slice in each glass. "Dig in."

Only too happy to oblige, she lifted a bite to her lips. Tasted.

"Oh, wow. It's delicious." The flavors steamed fragrantly on her tongue. "I'm going to warn you that cooking is the way to my heart, so tread carefully if you don't want me looking you up every time I'm hungry for polenta."

"Come over anytime." He lifted his fork toward her in mock salute. "I'll whip some up."

"You think I'm kidding," she managed to say between bites, enjoying the way the night wrapped around them, shielding them from the rest of the world. "But I fell in love with the way my third-grade boyfriend's mom made her peanut-butter-and-jelly sandwiches, and do you know I still crave those things? The secret is homemade bread. I'm pretty sure the peanut butter was homemade, too. She was a goddess."

Mrs. Hacking was also the kind of mom who hung her children's artwork on the walls in the most warm-hearted interior decorating Josie had seen to date, a direct contrast to her own mom, who admitted to having her in order to get the in-laws off her back about having a kid.

Josie forked up another bite, only too glad to bury that memory with Keith's cooking.

"So you were dating by third grade?" Keith asked as he helped himself to the polenta.

"Maybe I started too early, and that's what made

me gun-shy for the last couple of years." Recalling the
way her mom used to deck her out in designer fashions
at an early age, Josie shivered at the memory of being
paraded around like a sideshow at her parents' parties.
She pulled the blanket closer as a sea breeze stirred.

"Or maybe you've never found anyone whose cooking can compete with the third-grade mom."

"You cook *and* psychoanalyze?" Slipping another
bite of polenta into her mouth, she closed her eyes at
the warm comfort of delicious food. "One might cancel
out the other, now that I think about it."

"I'm much better at the former. An armchair pre-
tender at the latter. You want to psychoanalyze me over
polenta? Give it a shot. It's fun dinner conversation."

"Okay." Straightening in her seat, she assumed her
best German accent. "Can you tell me *anyfink* about
your dreams, Herr Murphy?" In a whisper, she added,
"I love games with accents. It's like decorating for your
voice."

"Actually, I'd been dreaming about numbers and balance sheets until I met a really hot brunette. I think I'm
going to dream about silver sequins tonight instead."

She straightened imaginary eyeglasses. "You have
verk on the brain. Very common. I prescribe vast
amounts of copulation and polenta."

Keith nearly lost his mouthful of water when she
said "copulation," but he swallowed without choking,
and laughed between coughs.

"I never got into the sexy doctor fantasy before," he
confided when he'd recovered. "But I think you just

introduced a whole new genre to my list of mental fa-
vorites."

"Glad to know I could pay you back for the food
somehow." She speared a forkful of fontina cheese and
sighed happily. "Who knew I could relax like this?"

"Cheers to that." He took another long drink of water.
"I really like my job, so I guess I haven't missed downtime, but I've had a damn good time today."

Peering across the table at the broad wedge of his
shoulders in his white T-shirt, she was amazed to think
she'd known him only for a day. A long, eventful day,
for sure. But still…she'd never gotten close to someone
so fast.

"I really like my job, too." She steered the conversation back toward work, figuring that was safer than
exploring how happy she felt. Tonight she just wanted
to enjoy the rare sense of well-being coursing through
her, so she concentrated on her meal, hoping she could
satisfy at least one hunger while she got to know him
better. "I think a lot of people don't get that, even people
who are in a position to pick and choose what they'd
like to do. Which is scary when you think about it—
how many people are out there doing jobs they don't
enjoy."

Keith shrugged, shoving aside his empty plate and
then moving to the other side of the table to sit next to
her. The action was quick and easy. The gesture touched
her, especially when he slid his arm around her shoulders. It all felt way too comfortable for how briefly
they'd known each other. But he followed her example

and took up the work thread, perhaps as eager as her to keep their conversation on more neutral terrain.

"People get trapped because they own a house and can't move when their company closes down. Or they have kids in school and don't want to leave a good district to follow a dream career." He poured more water into their glasses—clear plastic tumblers, which seemed a wise choice on board a watercraft. "Then again, maybe some folks just don't know themselves well enough to be able to figure out what sort of work they'd enjoy."

"I always knew I wanted to do something with art." Nearby, a fish jumped, a phantom splash in the water. It made her realize how long it had been since she'd heard any noise besides the gentle lapping of the waves.

"Like painting?"

"No. I stink at painting." She thought about how easy it would be to tip her head against his shoulder, to curl into the arm slung around her. "Yet I have definite opinions about what I like and what looks good next to a painting. The art of a house or the art of a room, I guess. But even before I got bitten by the interior design bug, I was working in fashion, creating wearable art."

"Fashion design?" The muscles in his shoulders tensed alongside hers. "As in European runway shows and four-thousand-dollar jackets?"

"Exactly. It's a whole different world." She still missed the all-night brainstorming on themes for collections, working side-by-side with brilliant fashion minds in an atmosphere of kinetic creative energy. "But if I'd made it in haute couture, I would have brought the same mantra to clothes that I'm now bringing to rooms—you don't have to spend boatloads of cash to surround yourself with beautiful things."

"Very egalitarian of you." He twined a lock of her hair around his finger and then spun it out again, watching it coil on her shoulder.

The action—so simple and yet sweetly intimate at the same time—gave her a warm, tingling feeling inside that had nothing to do with sexual chemistry. It was a warning sign, perhaps, that talking about work wasn't going to distract her from how very much she liked Keith Murphy.

"Thank you." Leaning forward, she started to stack the plates. "And I call cleanup duty, since you did the cooking."

If he was surprised by her abrupt need to hop to her feet and bustle around the makeshift table, he did a good job of concealing it. Maybe he was committed to keeping this trip free of complications, too.

"Deal." He picked up the tray when she had things stacked in the center. "I'll just carry this down for you. Then I've got a few text messages to send while we have sketchy connectivity. I can't make calls, but the texts are going through."

"We must be close enough to shore," she mused. "Hard to believe when it's so quiet out here."

But it was a good reminder that, no matter how isolated they felt, they weren't far from civilization. She might as well enjoy every moment of her time out here with Keith, because once they returned to the real world, he would take Green Principles global, while she remained in Boston to continue building her business.

With any luck, the tabloids would never learn that Josie had resurrected her inner party girl for this one, reckless outing.

R U sure U want to sell *Vesta*?

Keith typed out the message while seated on deck under the stars as Josie cleaned up in the galley. He hit Send, knowing his brother Jack had discovered his ex-girlfriend on the catamaran by now. Keith had sent him a warning that she was onboard to travel north to Bar Harbor, since the corporate boat was headed there anyhow. But, typical Jack, he'd ignored those texts and been completely surprised to find Alicia there.

Jack was still on the catamaran and hadn't sent Keith any rants about deceiving him into spending time with Alicia. A good sign, right?

His phone buzzed with a new message.

Wait on it. U can dock wherever.

Jack was having second thoughts about selling the boat that had been sentimental for him and Alicia. So much for the Charleston trip. Now Keith needed to decide whether to be honest with Josie and call it quits early on the minivacation. Or keep the news to himself and see what happened in the next two days.

Trying to set up a situation where he could walk the line without feeling like a heel with her, Keith clicked out a reply.

Front coming through. Will sail ahead for kicks & dock where it catches me.

That gave him an excuse to stay on the water longer. He sensed that, despite Josie's initial resistance to the trip, she was enjoying herself. And, damn it, she needed the vacation time as much as he did.

His phone vibrated again and he looked at Jack's final message.

Fine. But U still sail like crap.

Chuckling, Keith shut off the device without replying. No words were necessary, since they'd already had this debate at Ryan's engagement party. Obviously the former navy boy would never have handed over his precious sailboat if he didn't trust Keith in the first place. But every damn one of his brothers liked to talk smack. Even their honorary brother, Axel, a Finnish hockey player, who'd lived with the Murphys during his last year of high school. Six months out of Helsinki and he'd been as mouthy as the rest of them.

"You look rather amused." Josie's voice startled him as she emerged from the companionway close to where he sat on the rear deck.

The all-around light illuminated her delicate features,

revealing a hint of shadows under her eyes. He looped his arms around her neck, thinking he could carry her straight to his bed and tuck her in beside him. Maybe the gentle rocking of the boat would help lull him to sleep before he did something really selfish, like undress her again.

"My siblings are an endless source of entertainment." Rising, he met her before she reached the seats. "Thanks for putting away dinner. You must be exhausted. A good host would let you go to sleep now."

"An observant host would have noticed I never do anything by half measures once I commit myself." She lifted herself onto her toes to kiss him, her body skimming against his from hip to shoulder as she moved.

Thoughts of sleep vanished.

"That begs the question," he murmured, his hands roaming her back possessively, "what exactly are you committed to right now?"

She lifted a questioning eyebrow, an expression he was beginning to realize came right before one of her low-key zingers.

"Don't you remember? We're on a strict regimen of polenta and copulation to help us relax."

"Believe me. I didn't forget." He'd nearly choked on his tongue the first time she'd said it. "But I know this has been a long day and you didn't get much sleep last night."

"So we'll sleep in tomorrow." She tugged him toward the companionway and peered up at him with mischievous dark eyes.

"I guess I underestimated your level of dedication to, uh, relaxing."

"Remember how committed I was to decorating a boat? I risked travel sickness and stumbled through a strange marina at midnight to land that job." Carefully, she stepped backward to descend the stairs. "You can't imagine how much perseverance I have to offer this new program of enforced leisure."

His body promptly forgot he was working on just a few hours of sleep. His skin buzzed with a vibration so strong it was as if someone plugged a tuning fork directly into his nervous system.

Following her down the stairs into the main salon, he moved with her as they slowly made their way to the bow of the boat.

"I'm very good at alleviating stress." He watched as she stepped into the queen berth.

He'd replaced the trundle-bed mattress earlier, while he'd been cooking their late-night dinner. All the candles had been extinguished, so the space was dark except for a small hurricane lamp he'd left burning on the nightstand.

"What can you do for tension?" She batted her eyelashes and feigned innocence. "I've had this knot of coiled tension deep inside."

Stopping at the bed, she threw off the blanket she'd been using on deck. Now she wore a filmy purple top she'd bought at the boutique back on Nantucket.

"That sounds serious." Backing her up against the bed, he stepped between her legs, nudging apart her

feet, which were clad in the leather moccasins he'd purchased for her. "I'm going to need you to be very specific about the location of this tension so we can address
it."

She bit her lip. "You wouldn't believe me if I told
you."

Fire licked up his spine. "Try me."

"It's a female problem." She arched that eyebrow
meaningfully. "It's a bit awkward to explain, really."

"Hmm." His gaze roamed slowly over her as he savored the moment. Savored the sight of her with the
golden lamplight flickering on her skin. "I'd better take
a look."

He'd never been one for role-playing games, but then,
he'd never met a woman who could fall into a character
so easily and have so much fun with it.

"May I?" His hands went to the buttons on her blouse,
ready to slide the first fastening open. He couldn't wait
to see more.

"Of course." She lifted her chin. "I'm willing to sac-
rifice modesty if you can cure me."

She helped him pull off the blouse while it was still
half-buttoned, her impatience clear despite her turn as
an ailing Victorian maiden. He felt more than a little
impatient himself, his mouth watering for a taste of her.

"I see the first problem." Eyeing the soft swell of her
breasts above the edge of a black lace bra, he skimmed
a fingertip across one creamy mound.

She arched toward his touch. "I hope you won't keep

me in suspense," she urged, her hips brushing his in a twisting move to get closer.

He hooked a finger in the underwire of the bra, his knuckle pressing into her flesh. "I'd recommend you free these." Jiggling the lace gently, he enjoyed the show. "Lie back and I'll show you."

Breathing fast, she eased down onto the bed, her skin a pale contrast to the dark blue quilted spread. She looked so good, so ready for more, that he was tempted to simply pull off the rest of their clothes and sink deep inside her. But her game had gotten them ramped up in a hurry, and it didn't seem fair to stop just yet. Who knew how much hotter it might get before all was said and done?

Besides, if he could have a starring role in her future fantasies…he'd like that a whole lot.

Stretching out next to her, he freed the front clasp and pushed the lace cups aside. The tight rosebud nipples strained toward him and he captured one with his lips to draw on the tip. She sucked in a gasp and moved restlessly working her hips as if against an unseen lover.

"See? Doesn't that feel better already?" Keith asked, licking a path from one breast to the other.

"Yes and no," she whispered urgently, spearing her fingers through his hair to guide him to the other taut peak. "It feels good here, but it makes the other tension worse."

The tea rose scent of her skin and the way she moved worked on him like aphrodisiacs. The need to touch her was killing him, even though he'd had her twice in the last four hours.

"Show me," he said, placing his hand on her bare stomach right above the waistband of the jeans she'd tugged on before dinner. "Show me where and I'll take such good care of you."

Covering his hand with hers, she steered him lower. Then stopped.

"Will you help me with this?" She guided his palm to the zipper. "The place I'm taking you is well hidden."

The zipper pretty much went up in flames at his touch, the jeans vanishing in his haste. He left in place the black lace panties with a red satin heart, an act of restraint that damn near killed him.

"It's here." She guided his fingers lower, right over the red satin appliqué. Carefully separating his fingers, she directed two digits to the warmth between her thighs. "Right here."

Her voice broke on a ragged breath as he stroked her. She was so hot. So very responsive.

Slowly dragging his fingers up the lace-covered cleft, Keith could see her body flush with heat, her cheeks and breasts warm with color. Eyelashes fluttering, she turned her head this way and that, warring with the need that must have bitten her hard.

He could take this higher. Hotter. He knew that now, as her release hovered so close. But she'd been the one to make up this game, and she'd edged him to the brink.

Now it was her turn to benefit from a little sensual playtime.

"KEITH?"

Josie's eyes opened the moment his touch disappeared. Her heart was beating frantically, her breath a scarce commodity after being held for long stretches. How could a man make her forget to *breathe?*

"Right here," he assured her, shifting lower on the bed.

Lower still.

She blinked, a little confused, but not entirely surprised when his elbow wound up beside her knee. Heat flared inside her from some deep, sweet source. That position on the mattress could only mean...

"I'm already so close," she protested, not sure why he'd give her that kind of gift—was there any other term for oral sex?—when he already had her teetering on the brink.

"I know." He smoothed his palm over one hip, fingers dipping beneath the lace of her panties. "That's why I thought I'd better slow things down, to make sure you got every moment of pleasure you deserved."

The lace edged down her thigh, tickled her knees and then was gone. Utterly naked, she felt all the more bare because of her affinity with clothes. Fashion imparted a certain power. Identity. Even if nothing more than a snazzy pair of undies, clothes made a statement. Without hers, she couldn't work up the nerve to play a role or adopt a fun accent.

At her most vulnerable moment, Keith Murphy had the grace to stare at her body as if that alone had rendered him speechless. Touched, she gave herself over to the man and the moment, reclining on the mound of pillows piled at one end of the bed. Her eyelids drifted closed, the whirlwind of sensations spinning through her so fast she couldn't begin to comprehend them all.

His lips on her thigh startled her, the warm kiss a thrill that sent shivers up her spine. She peeked at him again, just for a moment, and melted to see the gentle reverence he used as he lavished attention on her there. His dark lashes fanned out above high cheekbones, his focus solely on her. Broad hands spanned her legs just above the knee, ready to shift or hold them as needed. Yet for now, he simply kissed her.

With that image emblazoned in her mind, she shut her eyes once more, to savor it. Josie dug her fingers into the bedcovers, wanting to have a hold on something as his mouth traveled upward in a serpentine path that veered inside her thigh and then back to the top of leg, landing on her bikini line.

Breathe, she reminded herself, stunned by the pleasure that shimmered beneath the surface of her skin. It held her enthralled, a magical spell making her body captive to Keith's touch.

His hands came alive then, shifting over her with restless caresses. They stirred the need in her, driving the sensations from pleasure to hunger as his fingers skimmed up the backs of her thighs to cup her bottom, urging her closer to his kiss.

A feline purr rumbled in her throat and she couldn't help the roll of her hips toward him, giving him access to what they both wanted. He answered with a tongue stroke up the center of her, a lightning strike to her very core. Whatever magic he was casting, they were bound by it now.

Melting against him, she swallowed another needy moan while the heat of his kiss seared her. The raw scrape of his evening stubble against her delicate thigh was a welcome contrast to the sweet slide of carnal kisses. Fingers twisting in the sheets, she knotted the bed linens, holding on for dear life while tension coiled inside her.

She wanted to tell him to bury himself deep within her before she lost all control. But she must have waited too long, because she couldn't catch her breath or pull back from the heady sensations.

When the tension finally released, she unwound like a spring into lush spasms. Sensual tremors undulated through her like waves, until the only thing keeping her together was Keith. He steadied her hips with his hands, pinned her legs with his body. His kiss urged her to that last high, wringing every last sweet contraction from her.

At last she stilled, spent beneath him. Only then did he break contact and slide away from her. She tugged her eyes open to see him shed the last of his clothes. He found a condom near the bed and rolled it on before returning to her side. She didn't want to protest, and yet she didn't know how much she could contribute to sex with her limbs so limp and heavy.

But then he covered her, his powerful shoulders

bunching and flexing as he moved up the bed, all male strength and virility.

Something stirred within her again, a warm and receptive feminine need. She wrapped her arms around his neck, arched closer. Her breasts met the hard wall of his chest, molding to him. He tilted her hips, making room for himself between her thighs. When he sank deep inside, she felt a sense of completeness that went beyond the physical connection. The rightness of the moment wrapped around her as surely as his muscular body.

Her gaze met his. Locked. Called by the need to mate with him on every level, she cradled his face in her hands and kissed him, tasted her passion on his lips.

The room around them disappeared, her focus narrowed to just this man. The sweet tension began inside her all over again, the same one that he had just released so expertly. Now, the pleasure built once more, surprising her with how swiftly it took her higher, and higher still.

She was falling deep into his green eyes and into the sensations he sparked throughout her long-dormant body. Gripping his shoulders, she clung to him, matching each thrust of his hips with an answering lift of her own. Too soon, the rhythm of that erotic dance took over. It didn't matter that she'd had an orgasm ten minutes ago. Another one built, demanded an outlet. Powerless to deny the passion, she worked her hips shamelessly against his, finding the right cadence to please them both until fulfillment rocketed through her.

Her release was so strong it made her dizzy. Hands splayed on Keith's back, she swayed with the force of those hungry feminine muscles as they throbbed all along his staff.

She knew when those contractions got to him. She could feel him stiffen even more, his shoulders going as rigid as the hard length inside her. Wrapping her legs around him, she drew him deeper for the ride, savoring the response he'd held off for her sake.

Pleasure seemed to carry them far away for long, timeless moments. It took half of forever to float back to consciousness. To take stock of the bed linens tangled around her limbs. At last her heartbeat slowed to a more reasonable rhythm and she realized she still clutched Keith's shoulders like a woman who never wanted to let go.

Carefully, she relaxed her hands, discomfited to discover how completely she'd let the moment take over. Her cheeks heated, a ridiculous reaction in light of all they'd just shared. Still, she hid her face against his chest and breathed in the warm, male scent of him.

If that was her unconscious reaction to sex with Keith, what might her conscious mind do two days from now, when she needed to go back to her real life?

Flexing her fingers to ease the gentle ache from holding him so tight, Josie decided that if they could spend all their time together in a horizontal position, maybe she'd stand a fighting chance of excising this insane hunger for him by then.

If not?

She'd have an incredibly fun time trying.

7

GETTING THE SHEETS just right on the sailboat was like putting the pedal to the metal on a sports car.

Keith howled with exhilaration as he felt the hull practically lift up out of the water to cut cleanly through the sea the next day. He had the vessel running hard and fast now, cruising just ahead of the oncoming storm front on the gusts of warm air.

And didn't that feel like an apt metaphor for his relationship with Josie? They were living for the moment, squeezing every bit of momentum out of this window of time before the waters got rough.

Call him a cynic, but the seas had a way of turning on you when you weren't expecting it. He just hadn't realized how much he'd missed walking that kind of tightrope until now. He'd put a lid on that need for adventure when he went to college, determined to prove himself in a way that set him apart from his highly competitive family. No more boat races and no more feats of strength; just focus on his studies and building his business. His relationship with Brooke had probably been a sign that his adventure seeking wasn't done, that he needed something else to fulfill that side of him, since the business world wasn't the place for anything but the most carefully calculated risks. But Brooke's social exploits had only been a diversion for the deeper need.

Sailing a reach was more his speed.

Securing the line on the jib before he took a seat, Keith lifted his face into the wind, his clothes plastered to his skin from the force of it. He'd come topside shortly after sunrise, needing the space to sort out his head after the night before. He hadn't spent so much one-on-one time with a woman in a long while and it messed with his mind to think how much he'd enjoyed the hours with Josie. Not just the sex, either. Although that had been in a class by itself in his experiences with women.

No, he'd had a great time *shopping* with her. His brothers would never let him live it down if he admitted something like that. Hell, he'd probably have to forsake the Murphy name. Of course, the dressing-room antics had elevated the outing from an average trip to the stores. But even when they'd just been strolling around Nantucket or sharing polenta at midnight, he'd had a rocking good time with Josie. Her ambitious nature and dedication to her work impressed him, but a fun-loving streak lurked just beneath the surface.

He could fall for a woman like that.

That's the part that had chased around his brain this morning when he'd been watching her sleep. He'd put the whole dating scene behind him after Brooke had taken him for a ride. Keith had no desire to get caught up in a relationship with anyone who was interested only in his name and family connections. Brooke's party-girl lifestyle had been carefully crafted to ensure she knew all the right people and got invited to all the right events. His family's wealth and global ties had been far more attractive to her than he ever had.

It was enough to sour a guy. But Josie had nothing in common with someone like her. Maybe the time had come to take a risk….

"Morning!" Josie surprised him as she shouted over the wind.

He looked up from his reverie and wondered how long he'd been staring vacantly at the horizon, thinking about her. She stood in the shelter of the companionway, holding her hair in one hand. Even though she'd fastened the dark locks back with a scarf, some strands whipped against her face from the speed of the watercraft.

"Morning?" he called back, his voice carrying more easily over the slap of water against the hull and the wind in the sails. He tapped the timepiece on his wrist. "Better check your clock."

"Hardly my fault I needed extra sleep after last night." Climbing up onto the main deck to sit beside him at the helm, she lifted her face to the sunlight. "Although I have to admit that sleeping until noon is my idea of vacation. Thank you for this."

She gestured to the water and sky that surrounded

them, while he steered to the port side to take best advantage of the shifting wind.

"It feels great to be out here, doesn't it?" His gaze moved from the horizon back to her. She wore an aquamarine blouse with jeans, along with the bright scarf tied gypsy-style around her hair.

"We're moving so fast today." She squinted at the dials on the helm. "It feels like flying."

"That's the warm front mixing with a cold front coming from the other direction. We've got a few hours before the storm hits. Until then, we'll be experiencing ideal conditions."

"Until then." She raised an eyebrow. "And how much advance warning will we have before 'then' arrives?"

"Just keep an eye out for clouds." He pointed overhead to blue sky stretching in every direction. "We'll see them off the stern before we feel a change in the weather."

"Will we have time to head inland?"

"Probably not. But I'd hate to sail too close to shore, since we'd lose the chance to really experience the thrill of the ride." It had been too long since he'd hit the open water like this. No way would he hug the shore just because of a few clouds in the distance. "Don't worry. I'll take good care of you."

"You're not one for playing it safe, are you?" She gave a wary glance behind them.

"No guts, no glory. There was talk of putting it on the Murphy family crest, actually." In fact, maybe that was his answer for these feelings for Josie. Maybe he needed to take a risk with her.

It jazzed him no end to think he was starting to know her so well in such a short time. Already he knew how and where she liked to be touched. He wondered how long it would take him to rev her up now, while she sat beside him, unaware of his sensual machinations....

"There's a Murphy crest?" She shifted, her shoulder brushing his in an incidental touch that belied all the ways they'd caressed one another the night before.

He answered it by grazing her thigh with his.

"Unofficially, yes." He relished the way her eyes flicked down to his leg. He was tempted to palm her thigh and follow through on the teasing brush of legs, but he reined himself in for the sake of continuing the game. Instead, he doled out a bit of Murphy family lore for entertainment value. "On the day of the annual Murphy Turkey Bowl, my dad flies his high-school football jersey from a post for a golf-flag post. He claims old number thirty-four is the family standard."

Not just in the medieval-crest sense, either. Dad truly figured his business achievements had set the bar for all his sons. Good thing Keith wasn't thinking about that, and had Josie's delectable body beside him to concentrate on. He leaned forward in his seat, ostensibly to check a gauge, to give himself a reason to increase the sweet friction between them.

"I remember reading an article in a regional business magazine about your dad, and it made some reference to a strong competitive streak." Her voice was a little breathless.

"You could say that." Keith steered to the starboard side to give an oncoming yacht more room. "One year my oldest brother, Ryan, wore that jersey of Dad's in the backyard game and I tore it when I tackled him. Tunnel vision prevented Dad from seeing the great play, focusing his attention solely on the shredded bit of his past glory."

"Uh-oh. Was your dad furious?" Josie edged closer to Keith as the wind picked up, and he wondered if she was onto the game he was playing. The side of her breast skimmed his chest for the briefest moment, making him forget about everything but the feel of her.

"Mostly there was a lot of grief about me not knowing the fundamentals of form tackling." The ass-chewing he'd received hadn't prevented Keith from playing hard in future games. "But it helped me to see that unless I made one hell of a big deal about my achievements, my father would never see them, anyhow. Since I don't have my youngest brother's finesse as an athlete, I turned to the business world to make my mark."

"You've certainly accomplished that," she assured him as a big superyacht cruised past them. Bass pumped from a sound system on the pool deck, where a couple of girls in bikinis danced in the sun.

They were nothing compared to the woman beside him, Keith thought. He couldn't even play a game of sexy touches with her without getting too turned on to win. Steadying the sailboat in the wake of the yacht,

Keith tried to recall what they'd been discussing, instead of thinking about the feel of her next to him. Oh yeah, his "accomplishments."

"You don't know my family," he told her finally.

"Seriously? With a company like Green Principles to your name, how can anyone dispute your success?" She frowned at the very idea.

Keith didn't need anyone to stand up for him. Never had. But he'd never guessed how cool it would be to know that someone *would.*

"My father owns properties all over the world. He's not easily impressed." Although a contract with Wholesome Branding would help. Their global ties would enable Green Principles to expand abroad.

Unfortunately, Keith knew he wouldn't be able to meet with the owner of Wholesome Branding during this trip as he'd originally hoped. Between Jack's about-face on the sale of the *Vesta* and Josie's limited time, a stop in Virginia was no longer an option.

"Well, that's ridiculous. He should be insanely proud to have raised someone with the foresight and business acumen to start a profitable company during a recession, and grow it by leaps and bounds in just a few years."

When the sailboat bounced on a choppy wave of the superyacht's wake, Josie slid into him, her hip soft against his. Her proximity made him slow to process what she'd said.

"Did I tell you about the growth margin?" Though it was true, he didn't remember bragging to her.

Her cheeks brightened. "I might have looked you up on Google while we were in Nantucket."

He told himself that was normal. Natural. People did it all the time with individuals they were dating, or doing business with. And yet...

Experience with Brooke had made him wary. Their families did business together, but Brooke had pushed for the first date to strengthen the tie and further her social connections. She'd admitted as much later in their relationship, never suspecting how off-putting he found it to be singled out for such superficial reasons.

"Are you offended?" Josie seemed surprised by his silence, straightening in her seat.

"Of course not." He scavenged for words that would smooth over the moment, and couldn't find the right ones.

"But it obviously makes you uncomfortable to think I was checking you out."

"No." Damn it. With an effort, he forced Brooke's shallow behavior from his mind. "You're smart to find out what you can about a guy who invites you for a date in the middle of the Atlantic. I only hesitated because I have an ex who researched her dating prospects. She wasn't looking out for her safety, though. She was looking for a good time. Brooke was more of a jet-set party girl."

Josie's face drained of color, and for a moment, Keith thought maybe the choppy wake had brought back her motion sickness.

"Are you okay?" He let go of the controls, allow-ing the customized self-steering mechanism to kick in while he rested a steadying hand on her shoulder.

She shook her head, the tail of her silk scarf brushing her cheek. "There's something you ought to know about the whole jet-set, party-girl thing. Because the truth is, I have that in common with your ex."

JOSIE WATCHED as Keith's expression hardened.

His mouth flattened into a line. The hand that had been resting on her shoulder disappeared. And was it her imagination, or had the sky grown darker, too?

The whole day felt a little more ominous somehow.

They still sailed fast through open water, the boat recovering an even keel after being bounced around by the mammoth yacht. But Josie's insides continued to flounder, her nerves taut after Keith's surprise admission about his ex.

She could only imagine what he was thinking. She was struggling enough with the abrupt shift from totally turned on to stunned by Keith's news.

"I don't understand." He backed up a fraction, inserting a space between them where there hadn't been any before. "You're a hardworking, ambitious businesswoman—"

"With a past reputation for being a fixture on the society pages." She didn't say it to brag, since her former presence there had nothing to do with her and everything to do with her wealthy family.

"In that case, I'm surprised I didn't recognize your name."

She could see him trying to relax, shaking the tension out of his shoulders. But even his tone of voice told her that his guard was still up.

"I changed it legally three years ago when I started the interior design business. Passano is my mother's maiden name. My father's name is Davenport." Josie didn't miss the light of recognition in his eyes. "That rings more bells, doesn't it?"

And—she'd be willing to bet—not in a good way.

"It's a well-known family name," he hedged, possibly looking for something positive to say. "I think there were Davenports in my fifth-grade history book."

"There probably were." She felt a hot, itchy sensation up the back of her neck and wondered how many people in the world could claim a discussion about their parents made them break out in hives. "I have to look back that far on the family tree to find any evidence of ambition, but obviously it existed at one time for Cornelius Davenport to have accumulated enough of a fortune to finance the next five generations of trust-fund babies. Excuse me, make that *four* generations, since I've weaned myself off the family gravy train."

In the distance, she thought she heard a rumble of thunder, but she was no longer so concerned about the storm catching up to them. A nice cold downpour might ease the self-consciousness that came with introducing her past to Keith now that she understood he had an aversion to pampered jet-setters.

She'd thought she'd been safe to indulge in this time with him as long as they kept it private. She hadn't thought that Keith would find her a pariah once he learned her true identity.

"Access to the family fortune doesn't put you in the same category as my ex," he insisted, apparently still giving her the benefit of the doubt.

"No. But club hopping with vacuous trendsetters in the hope of getting some attention in the press—that qualifies, right?" No sense putting a happy face on it. She'd done just that to promote her fledgling fashion career, prowling around the clubs in her designs, initiating conversations about clothes wherever possible.

The growl of thunder increased until Keith rose to his feet for a better look at the sky to the north. She turned, too, seeing the clouds there—swiftly changing ones that even as she watched seemed to be rolling closer. The air crackled with the tension between them, but that would have to wait until more practical concerns had been addressed.

"This is coming up quicker than I expected. I've got to hoist the storm sail." He checked some gauges and then tapped a screen on the helm that looked like radar or GPS. "While I take care of that, I need you to keep us on course, okay? I'll be able to see any oncoming traffic, so don't worry about that, just steer toward this dark spot on the map. It's shallow there. A little island off the coast."

She was about to remind him she'd never driven a boat before, but he'd already leaped out onto the deck to tend to the complicated spiderweb of lines that corresponded to the various sails. His haste as he moved from one spot to the next made her think he had his hands full with storm prep, so she kept her eye on the dark blob on the map, and tried to make sure she steered toward it.

He worked quickly and efficiently, raising one sail and lowering another, his broad shoulders and defined arms flexing with the constant movement. He angled the storm sheets to take full advantage of the wind from the oncoming storm, so their speed continued unabated. Josie didn't know anything about sailing, but with the way he moved from one task to the next, she guessed he was damn good at it.

If she hadn't known he was only waiting to dock to give her a premature heave-ho, now that he'd recognized her as exactly the kind of woman he did not want, she might have actually enjoyed the day. Unlike those scary times on the boat with her parents, now she was with someone who knew what he was doing. Someone who could take on Mother Nature and win.

What a hell of a time to realize how much she admired Keith's ambitious desire to conquer the world—or the sea—with his own two hands. Their race through the water didn't require big engines or high-end technology, although as a newbie navigator she was grateful for the blinking map to guide her steering. This trick with the sails had been done the same way by people for thousands of years, harnessing the wind to skim over the water. What a thrill to take on the wild gusts whipping across the deck.

But as much as she liked the electric spark in the air,

she regretted that the storm's arrival meant they'd have to go ashore, mark an end to a crazy adventure. And now that Keith knew about her past, he wouldn't even spare her a backward glance. Though that had been the plan all along, she realized she would sorely regret not getting to know Keith Murphy much, much better.

8

THE DARK CLOUDS CAUGHT UP to them at the perfect time.

Keith was only too glad to race around the deck like a madman, raising the storm sail and squeezing every last bit of speed from the boat to make it to a marina on the coast of Block Island. Hell, he was an expert at burying his problems in work, after all. That tendency was one of the reasons he headed up his own multimillion-dollar company now.

Since there were no lucrative deals to close on board the *Vesta,* he spun his excess energy—his gut-twisting response to Josie's revelation—into sailing the vintage vessel for all it was worth. Because damn, once they dropped anchor at the marina, he'd be faced with either saying his goodbyes to Josie or digging deeper with her to see what she meant about her partying lifestyle.

As he trimmed the storm jib a bit more and felt the first fat raindrop hit the back of his hand, he admitted that both options sucked. He would have preferred to wait out the weather holed up in some coastal cottage with Josie, exploring every conceivable pleasure they could dream up in the next twenty-four hours, until he had to face facts.

That she manipulated friends for the sake of their connections? That she wanted to be the center of attention everywhere she went so people would remember her name?

That didn't sound like Josie. Yet by her own admission…

The rumble of thunder yanked his thoughts to the present as a wall of rain moved toward them.

The weather was changing fast.

"Keith!" Josie shouted from behind the helm. She stood, her blue-and-yellow scarf whipping in the wind as she pointed to the gray torrent marching across the waves, closer and closer.

The water swelled beneath the *Vesta,* lifting the fiberglass hull high before smacking it back down, sending Keith's feet out from under him.

Crap. His knees hit the deck with a thud. He rose to his feet in time to see Josie still standing, clinging to the steering mechanism, which must have been what kept her upright.

"Are you all right?" He scrambled beneath the rigging to reach her, finding the deck drenched from spray.

Her knuckles were white where she clutched the wheel, her clothes drenched with seawater. He dug inside a locker to retrieve floatation devices for them as a precaution. Yanking one over his head, he slammed the door shut and brought the other to Josie. He reached her in time to bolster her through another high wave, his body cleaving to hers instinctively, shielding her from the worst of the vicious back spray.

When the wave tipped the boat down again, he was ready for it, anchoring them with one hand on the rail while he locked her waist to his hips. He kept his knees bent, ready for impact.

"Can you believe it?" Josie gasped, turning to peer up at him, her dark eyes alight.

Almost as if…she was enjoying this?

"Are you okay?" he asked again, realizing how tightly he gripped her, his hand molded to her ribs through the thin fabric of her wet blouse.

The feel of her delicate curves reminded him that he needed to keep her safe. Belatedly, he dropped the other floatation device over her head and buckled the straps securely.

"I'm fine." She nodded quickly, turning to look back out to sea while Keith took over the steering. "Here it comes!"

She pointed toward the rainstorm moving steadily toward them like a cloud of locusts. She gripped his forearm, her fingers clenching hard as if to hold him tight through the storm.

He followed her gaze and watched as the downpour hit the rail, the seat cushions, and then drummed into their skin. It enveloped the boat in moments, sweeping in like a wet curtain.

With a squeal and a laugh, Josie tipped her face to the deluge, taking the onslaught head-on as they bobbed and dipped over the waves. She opened her mouth, tasting the torrent on her tongue as it soaked their clothes.

Keith watched her, absorbing the sight of her tucked under his arm. A rivulet of water streaked from the corner of her closed eye down her temple; her lashes were soon spiked with rain. Her scarf went limp, clinging damply to the dark strands of her hair.

With nothing to do but to ride the storm until they caught sight of safe harbor, Keith turned her in his arms, drawn to her in spite of the secrets she'd kept from him. Right now, there was just the two of them, fused together by shared body heat against the cold seawater splashing overboard and the downpour beating on their shoulders.

The realization that she enjoyed the adventure shook him harder than the incessant waves. The quirky fashion designer turned decorator didn't mind an occasional storm. In fact, judging by the gleam in her dark eyes, Keith would guess she was savoring it.

"These waves ought to put to rest any question of motion sickness for you," he said finally, too rocked by this new view of her to share any of his real thoughts.

Wind whipped across the deck, tugging at the damp scarf in her hair until she peeled the silk off and pocketed it.

"I feel more in control now than when I used to go out on the water with my parents. I think that helps." She gripped his shoulders as the boat lurched sideways. "At least, I know *you're* in control."

He recalled her story about her parents mixing cocktails on the deck of their boat and her worrying about them going overboard when she was a kid. That would account for enough anxiety to make her ill on a boat in the past. For that matter, remembering that story gave him an idea where her jet-set lifestyle came from. Maybe those choices weren't of her own making if she'd grown up in that kind of environment.

"Not just me. You're helping," he acknowledged. "I couldn't have raised the storm sails without you here." They made a good team, he thought, even if he didn't say it. Even if they couldn't carry their collaboration over into the real world.

The next wave hit with no warning. The deck dropped away beneath their feet and they fell together.

Keith kept his arm around Josie, buffering her. He watched the mast tilt awkwardly.

"What can I do?" Josie shouted through the din of rain.

He raced to snag a tether line and anchor it to her life vest. Sailboats were great in heavy weather, but he wasn't taking any chances with her.

"Try to stay on course." He gave her a quick squeeze before he released her. "And make sure to keep one hand on the rail to steady yourself."

"Got it." Nodding, she focused on the helm while he rushed toward the rigging to adjust the storm sheets.

They could always sail into the wind and wait out the storm, but with Block Island close by and the marina easily accessed, he preferred to get on shore for the night.

As much fun as it might be for them to ride the waves, he wouldn't press his luck.

He lost track of time as he handled the sheets, making frequent adjustments to keep the *Vesta* on course. Finally, Josie called to him through the rain, waving the shipboard radio to show that she was speaking to someone. Her wet clothes fit her like a second skin, the trim life jacket she wore doing too damn little to hide the appeal of her curves.

"It's the marina. They said we'll have to draft!" she shouted over the howling wind, her hand on the mouthpiece. "But they have room for us in the marina."

Not exactly an ideal situation, but he'd take it. Keith hoped Jack kept extra bumpers on board, since that meant they'd be sharing a slip with another boat.

"Get a slip number," he instructed, striding toward her to…peel those wet clothes off? No, damn it, he was there to double-check their heading. Forcing his brain back into gear, he added, "Tell them to have a dockmaster meet us. We're going to need help if we don't have much room to work."

Nodding, she relayed the message, while he looked at the map over her shoulder. She'd done a good job navigating, all things considered. He'd thrown her in without much guidance, but she'd kept things on course like a seasoned first mate in spite of the downpour. He made a quick adjustment as she finished her call to shore.

"It's slip 205," she reported, standing on her toes to see up over the deck to the horizon. "Should we be watching for traffic if we're close to the marina?"

He grinned in spite of their speed, the storm and the ominous cloud of unspoken issues that hovered between them. He'd pegged her for a workaholic right from the start, and sure enough, he gave her a job to do and she worked her tail off at it. Surely there had to be some reasonable answer to his questions about her partying past.

"I leave you alone here for fifteen minutes, and suddenly you're seizing command?"

Her eyes snapped back to his. "I'm sure I've read somewhere that a good captain keeps a lookout. And this boat is not going down on my watch."

"Mine neither," he protested, indulging his desire to touch her by stroking a finger down one side of her face. "My brother will go into heart failure if anything happens to the *Vesta,* for one thing. Not to mention I'll never hear the end of it if my sailing skills prove subpar."

She nodded, never cracking a smile. And he knew something had her worried. Probably not the storm, since she'd embraced the waves and the rain like an old sea captain. Could she be thinking about the end of their relationship? Funny how he could read her mood even without her uttering a word. That said a lot about how well he'd gotten to know her in a very short time.

"Hey." He tipped her chin up, to find her skin soft and cool beneath his fingertips. "Everything is going to be fine. We're almost there now and I'll have help tying up the boat. We made incredible time, traveling so far through weather like this."

"Where are we?" she asked, a hint of exasperation leaking through. "Where are we going? The digital maps are about impossible to read through all the rain."

"Block Island." He ran his thumb along the column of her throat, not wanting her to worry. "Off the coast of Rhode Island."

"And you really think we need to give up and head to shore?" She peered up at the sky as if a stray ray of sunshine might penetrate the thick clouds.

Did she ask out of concern for what was safest? Or was she reluctant about ending their trip together?

"Docking is a good option." Rechecking the GPS his brother had installed as an upgrade, Keith realized he needed to slow down and motor the rest of the way in. "The *Vesta* can weather the swells and the rain, but if the wind picks up, it could get even worse. We'll be on dry land soon and I can find a flight back home for you by tomorrow if you want. Okay?"

The reminder of the time limit on their relationship didn't put him at ease, even though he knew now that was probably wisest. His gut twisted unexpectedly at the thought of letting her go. Of never again feeling her soft body writhe under him, or never seeing her come unraveled in his arms, flushed and replete.

"What can I do?" she asked again, swiping away a trail of water sliding down her forehead toward one eye.

With the rain plastering a dark strand of hair against her cheek, Keith knew she couldn't share much in common with his ex-girlfriend no matter what she said. Brooke would have simply taken the sound system below deck during a storm, making sure the party didn't stop because of the rain. It never would have occurred to her to help him sail a boat. For that matter, she wouldn't have set foot on a vessel that wasn't navigated by a hired professional crew. Brooke and manual labor didn't mix.

Josie steered them onward and embraced the adventure.

He took a deep breath. "You can forgive me for thinking you were anything like my former girlfriend." He dropped a quick kiss on Josie's cheek. "Keep up the good work steering. We're almost there."

LIFTING HER HAND to her face, Josie touched the spot where Keith had kissed her. Not even the cold spray from a rogue wave could take away the warmth from that place. The deeper heat it inspired in spite of everything.

Squinting through the downpour to the GPS display that showed their direction, she bided her time while he took down the storm sheets and switched to engine power for more control as they docked. They motored slowly toward shore, features of which took shape out of the mist that had rolled over them after the rain started.

Her role was minimal, as two men from the marina came out to help Keith tie up the boat. Apparently "drafting" meant sharing a spot with another vessel, but according to one of the dockworkers, the other boat belonged to an older couple who took it out only occasionally. So Keith wouldn't need to worry about moving the *Vesta* until the storm passed.

Josie sat, somewhat comfortably, under a canopy Keith had found that snapped over the cockpit area to keep the captain—her, in this case—dry. Her clothes were still soaked, but it was easier to see the controls without raindrops streaking across them. Besides the GPS, she could read the speed setting.

Not bad for a reformed party girl. She had the impression that Keith was pleased with her efforts to get them through the storm, because ever since he'd planted that kiss on her cheek an hour ago, he'd been casting her sly glances that made her blood simmer. Besides, he'd said she was nothing like his ex—a statement that apparently meant good things—and that had warmed her in a different way.

All in all, she couldn't wait to see what the rest of the day held in store for them.

Now, his green eyes roamed over her as he tipped the dockworkers and assured them he and Josie would be ashore shortly. Apparently, he'd booked a suite in a hotel here, if the waves became too high for them to ride out the storm on the sailboat. She'd discerned that much by careful eavesdropping through her canvas hideaway.

Maybe the idea of going their separate ways tomorrow was messing with his head as much as it was hers. She knew one thing—she was going to make the most of tonight, with the possibility of saying goodbye looming.

The marina was shrouded in mist, a few buildings looming through the fog. Their slip was the farthest out, with nothing but ocean on their port side. To the starboard, a big yacht with the shades pulled tight blocked most of their view, although Josie could see the tops of a few masts through the grayness. They bobbed eerily, seemingly disconnected from any watercraft.

Peering through the plastic window in the canopy, she watched Keith stalk toward her in the rain, his dark T-shirt plastered to his skin in a way that revealed every striation of muscle along his chest and abs. With his dark hair slicked to his head, he had a dangerous look to him. Although part of that might be the fact that he hadn't shaved in a while.

It was a look that worked for him. He could have swapped places with his hockey star brother in a heart-beat, because right now he appeared every inch the tough-guy athlete ready to take his gloves off and rumble at the slightest provocation. Mostly he looked sexy and very, very male. Steam drifted up from his back and shoulders, the weather cooling him off after all his hard work to tie up the boat.

"Josie?" he called through the canopy. "Do you want to check in at the marina's resort to dry off?"

Noting the way his eyes dipped to travel leisurely over her body, she guessed he had some ideas in mind for the hotel. But she'd spotted the building on shore before the worst of the mist rolled in, and it looked like a long walk through the rain to get there. Too long to wait to put her hands on him.

"Not especially." She sauntered closer to the clear plastic, which functioned as both a window and a door. Pulling off a few snaps, she stepped through. "With all the heated looks pinging around here and warming me up, I think I'd like to get wet."

She meant getting wet in the rain. Truly, she did. But, that was *so* not what Keith heard. She could tell by the way his eyes narrowed as he strode forward, zeroing in on her like a homing device.

"That is…" She thought about explaining but the heat simmering between them proved too mesmerizing. Sultry.

She was pretty sure the raindrops that fell on her skin evaporated on contact, because she didn't notice them. She saw only the man in front of her. Felt only the magnetic pull of attraction.

"I'm right there with you." His arms went around her, eliminating the need for words.

Whatever misunderstandings remained between them would still be there later; she didn't doubt it for a minute. But she'd come on this trip with Keith to indulge herself, and she planned to make the most of every stolen moment while they had the privacy to explore this explosive heat.

Rising up on her toes, she kissed him. Rain sheeted down her back, soaking her shirt again and providing a cold contrast to the heat of his chest against her breasts, the molten possession of his lips. Closing her eyes and her thoughts to everything else, she gave herself over to his touch.

Broad hands spanned her waist, smoothed down her hips. He pulled her hard against him, molding her curves to fit the stark, unyielding planes of all that taut muscle, while his tongue stroked hers, claiming her.

Her knees turned rubbery and failed to hold her up. She would have fallen if not for his strong arms keeping her right where he wanted her. Her head spun with images of all the ways they could pass the rest of the day together, all the ways they could explore each other....

Keith seemed to have unleashed her inner sex goddess, a facet of herself she had not guessed existed until he touched her. She couldn't imagine walking away from this. From him. But with their time together quickly running out, she broke their kiss to venture a request in his ear.

"Let's stay on board," she whispered, her tongue darting out to catch a raindrop rolling along the lobe. "I've been having a major pirate fantasy..."

"Is there ravishing involved?" His words were a soft vibration against her throat as he kissed his way down her neck.

Answering shivers trembled through her and they didn't have a thing to do with the rain.

"Constant ravishing," she confided, tipping her head back to better feel the heady combination of his hot tongue and the cold raindrops sliding over her skin, down into the hollow between her breasts. "I'm very innocent and this pirate in my fantasy is insatiable for my—"

He hauled open the front of her blouse, sending buttons popping and rolling over the deck. Cupping her breasts in his hands, he slipped his thumbs inside the demi-cups of her yellow lace bra.

A hungry whimper escaped her lips as he circled each tip, teasing her into incoherence. Which was fine, since he obviously needed no further instruction on how to play the conquering pirate.

Lips fastening onto one nipple, he drew the tight crest into his mouth. Waves rocked the boat as the storm picked up force. She could have stayed there forever, captive to that seductive kiss, but he hoisted her up in his arms and carried her across the deck to the companionway. Blinking her eyes open, she met his gaze, a laser-hot force that melted her insides.

Confident he understood exactly what she needed, she allowed her head to tip into the crook of his arm, taking shelter against his body. He descended the short steps below deck in two strides, bringing them into the protected salon where they'd made love the first time.

He set her on her feet, only to make quick work of removing her clothes. Kissing her, he held her fast while he tugged off her scarf and the remains of her shredded blouse. Her fingers pulled at his T-shirt, rolling it up until she had to break their kiss to yank the damp fabric over his head. Sopping clothes fell away as he walked her backward, kissing, nipping, touching. She went for the fastening of his cargo shorts just before they reached the queen berth, but he restrained her wrists in a grip that reminded her of his pirate status.

Her skin tightened in response and a new wetness warmed her thighs. She'd never responded so fully, so quickly to any man. But Keith Murphy had her number, taking her fleeting fantasies and wringing the most mileage possible from them.

"Keith…" She wanted to tell him how he affected her, but the moment overwhelmed her.

She could only follow where the feelings took her.

Tumbling her onto the bed, he slid down her body and unfastened her jeans with his teeth. His tongue licked her navel, circling inside in a prelude to what might come next. She twisted beneath him, ready for more, captive to his whims. All the fantasies she'd had about him undressing her like this came flooding back, infusing the moment with a surreal quality that made it feel both dreamlike and real.

Her skin quivered, her legs shook with need as he stared down at her. She reached for him as he started to undress, her fingers strangely numb, since all sensation seemed concentrated in her breasts and between her legs.

He paused in the middle of unzipping his fly, and reached into the pocket of his shorts. Emerging with the long, damp length of scarf she'd worn on her head earlier, he tugged it free and wound it around her wrists like silk handcuffs. He didn't tie the ends, not really binding her but providing a tangible reminder of the fantasy she'd requested.

"Hold still," he warned in her ear, his breath hot and sultry on her skin.

"I can't wait anymore," she whispered, her whole

body on fire. "I'm not nearly as innocent as I pretended so, um—"

He cupped her sex in one palm, rendering her speechless while sensation swamped her. Her eyelids fluttered, but she wanted to watch him. His gaze was magnetic as he held her gently with one hand while using the other to finish undressing.

Fingers played over her slick folds, taking her higher than she ever believed possible. She thought she'd fly apart, but he stopped just before she came, and deliberately rolled on a condom. Next time, she'd pay him back for making her wait. But right now, she planned to savor every second of her ravishment.

He climbed over her, parting her thighs with one knee before he entered her in one heady stroke. Lights flashed behind her eyelids and she wondered if she might pass out. She looped her arms behind his head, her wrists still joined by the scarf. The ends of the silk trailed over his back to skim her arms while he moved inside her.

No one had ever been so good to her, so thoughtful of her needs and her wants. In two days, Keith Murphy had been kinder and more considerate of her than anyone she'd ever met. Emotions scattered inside her, a shotgun blast of feelings that spread everywhere. Then the sensual pleasure ramped up another notch, the storm inside her ready to break.

She didn't know where to put all the feelings—her body and soul were at this man's mercy in ways that didn't have anything to do with a flimsy scarf. Josie squeezed him tight, wrapping her legs around him and holding him close with her arms.

Her release rolled over her like a rogue wave, washing sweet sensation through her time and time again. Her hips arched against his and she fitted herself to him, taking every inch of him inside. The hard length of him throbbed with his own release, and she knew a primal disappointment at the latex barrier between them. In that insane moment, she wanted to feel the hot flood of his pleasure against her womb, to wring every last drop of fulfillment from him.

As it was, she settled for kissing him, connecting with him that way as she longed for another, impossible kind of connection. Some far-off part of her brain tried to assure her that was just biology. Or chemistry. Surely there was some scientific rationale for why she would feel so strongly about someone she'd just met.

Any other explanation simply wasn't possible. And yet…

The bliss of her release remained in her bloodstream like a drug, bringing endorphins to every corner of her physical being. She sprawled in the rumpled bed linens like a sated goddess—or a well-ravished maid—and wondered how she would ever disentangle herself from this man.

Prying one eye open to take in his strong profile in the dim cabin, Josie acknowledged she couldn't. Not yet.

She didn't know where this wild madness was taking her, but she couldn't relinquish it—or him—so soon.

They'd ridden out the storm together. Surely that meant they could weather another day or two without crashing on the rocky relationship shores that had already lashed him once.

Of course, Keith had practice keeping himself distant and holding back, after that experience with his ex. Whereas Josie had no idea how to accomplish such a feat. But with the inevitable reminder that taking their romance public would be hell on their careers, she should be fine, right?

9

THE RAIN EASED as the chartered flight touched down at Chatham Municipal Airport the next afternoon. Keith had heard that the weather was better to the northeast, and sure enough, the skies were clearing in Chatham.

The last thing he had wanted to do was leave the *Vesta*.

He'd had the most incredible two days of his life on board with Josie. But the morning after the storm, he couldn't offer her much beyond a lift home, since sailing was no longer an option with the front heading south. The evening before, after the stunningly intense sex on board the boat, they'd moved to the hotel. All night they'd indulged each other, communicating solely through touches and tastes, and yet somehow remaining in perfect concord. Then, by the gray light of dawn, they'd agreed to catch a flight back to Cape Cod.

"Any luck getting through to Chase?" he asked Josie as they disembarked.

She pulled a wheeled overnight bag behind her, the

one they'd bought in Nantucket just the day before yesterday. Somewhere in that bag lurked a silver sequined outfit that had driven him wild, but her black blazer and gray gabardine pants didn't give any hint of that playful side of her. He took the bag from her as they walked toward a waving driver from a local car service. The benefit of a tiny airport was that they could be off the plane and under way quickly.

"Yes. He says he'll meet us at your parents' place." She tucked her cell phone back into her purse and made a face, indicating she thought that was presumptuous on the guy's part. "Is that okay?"

Keith paid the driver in advance and left him to handle the bags while he got the door of a big Lincoln Town Car for Josie.

"It's fine. My mother's always glad to have people in the house."

"Does she *know* my cousin?" Josie frowned as she slid into the backseat. "My very distant cousin, I might add?"

"Sure. He graduated with Jack. In such a small town—with a small high school—you get to know everybody." Keith settled in beside her and pulled the door shut just as the driver fired up the engine.

"Well, I appreciate you letting us meet there, but I'll try to convince him to take me over to the marina so I can see his boat firsthand and finish up the deal I was trying to negotiate with him." She peered out the window, studying the scenery as they headed out toward the coast, where Keith had grown up.

Their driver took a phone call on his Bluetooth, his voice inordinately loud as he discussed the details of a future fare with a dispatcher or boss. Keith used the noise as a cover to speak more privately to Josie.

"For what it's worth, I hope you know I'm glad that you didn't board the right vessel that night." He had the sense he was losing her today. Not just because they were back on the mainland, but also because she'd retreated to her work clothes. She'd been glued to her PDA every moment of the flight that hadn't restricted electronic devices.

The joking, role-playing temptress he'd gotten to know on the boat seemed like another woman entirely.

She glanced up at him now as she tucked the PDA into her bag. "Me, too," she admitted. "It was good for me to get away from work for a while. I'm glad you talked me into a vacation."

Not exactly a declaration of undying devotion, but he didn't know what he'd expected.

"Look, I know you want to keep this thing light between us and you're committed to your career and all that. But I can't help thinking there might be more to us than just a fling." He put his cards on the table, not caring that the driver of the Town Car could glean a boatload of local gossip if he paid any attention. Besides the conversation on the Bluetooth, the kid had an earpiece to an iPod in one ear, and Keith could hear the rap tunes all the way in the back.

If the guy could decipher their conversation through all that noise, he deserved a second career as a superspy, although his job as a driver wouldn't last long if he insisted on skirting the road rules with the headphones.

"Umm." Josie glanced meaningfully at the kid and lowered her voice. "I don't think that's wise, especially since we never got around to that discussion that was brewing yesterday. You know, about the social circles in my past?"

"We can talk about it if you want, but I already told you that doesn't matter to me. I know enough about you to realize that I want to know you better."

She was already shaking her head, clearly wanting to interrupt. But he brushed a finger over her lips to quiet her.

"Josie, my business is based out of Boston and so is yours. We're going back to the same town after we tie up loose ends in Chatham. I think it's going to be tough to stay out of one another's way and just forget this ever happened. Frankly, I don't want to." He kept his voice low, too, more for her sake than concern about the driver, who was keeping time to a bass beat, thumping his hands on the steering wheel.

She bit her lip. Worried her teeth along the plump softness. He tried not to be insulted that the decision remained so difficult for her after everything they'd shared.

"I don't want to make trouble for you, and I'm nervous about meeting with Chase as it is. Can we wait and talk later? Maybe I can buy you dinner before I head back to Boston tonight."

"Yes to dinner, but you stand no chance in the battle

for the check." He gave her knee a playful squeeze to soften the he-man stance, from which there was no backing down. "That's just fair warning."

The car listed as the driver took the turn up the long driveway to Keith's parents' house.

"I can't exactly cook for you the way you did for me," she protested. "I have no kitchen in town so I'm at a distinct disadvantage...." She trailed off as they reached the sprawling, cedar-sided home his father had custom built in the mid-eighties. "Wow. I've seen it in a decorating magazine before, but it's even more impressive in person. And the gardens have all grown in so beautifully."

While her attention was divided, Keith took full advantage.

"So I'll drive us back to Boston tonight after your meeting with Chase. We can take your car and grab dinner on the way. You'd really be helping me out, since I took my boat down here for Ryan's engagement party and my car is back in Boston."

"Sure." She nodded absentmindedly. "I hate driving at night. Look at the all the peaks and windows. I love shingle-style homes. It's got the atmosphere of a seaside cottage, blending right into the landscape, and yet it's so huge." She kept up a running commentary about the home as the driver stopped the car and brought their bags to the door.

Keith tipped him while Josie admired a hedge of some bright red bushes and complimented the ground cover between the flagstones, of all things. Apparently, meeting her on a boat, he hadn't been properly introduced to her decorator side. He'd bet next year's profits that his mom was going to adore her.

The thought put a smile on his face until he realized how inordinately happy the notion made him. He was starting to care about Josie a lot in a short amount of time. Giving anyone that much power, so quickly, put him on edge.

That concerned him, since she'd agreed to share a ride back to Boston only because she didn't like driving at night and was distracted by the house. Memories of her biting her lip in indecision returned.

But all those issues evaporated temporarily when the main door to his parents' house opened. Expecting to see his mother's sleek blonde bob and welcoming arms, he wasn't prepared for a man's lanky frame leaning against the doorjamb, dressed head to toe in black designer fare.

Chase Freeman had taken it upon himself to welcome them in person.

"Hello, beautiful." He reached to embrace Josie, kissing her on the cheek with a warmth that didn't appear one bit familial from where Keith was standing. "Sorry I missed you the other night."

He held her a fraction too long, making the hair stand up on Keith's neck like a damn dog's.

It helped somewhat that Josie's expression on the other side of Chase's shoulder suggested she found the man odious in the extreme. But Keith resented the fact that she felt the need to work for anyone she didn't like.

"Keith?" The soft, feminine voice of his mother came from somewhere within the house.

"We're here, Mom," he called, tempted to bulldoze right through Freeman, except that the guy hadn't fully released Josie yet. "Sorry for the short notice. And, Chase? Man? Your *cousin* would like to breathe again sometime today."

Still the guy took his time letting her go, before making a big production of presenting her with a folded piece of paper.

"The contract?" Josie took it and unfolded it.

"Plus a check. Half now, half on completion, right?" He tugged her hair as if she were an eight-year-old, bugging Keith more than a little.

Thankfully, his mother made her way into the foyer and by her presence alone forced the jerk-off to show some manners. Introductions were made all around and, as Keith had predicted, Josie hit upon one of Colleen Murphy's favorite subjects right away—the house. His mother warmed to her immediately, insisting on showing the decorator her favorite features and rooms, leaving Keith in the hall with Chase Freeman, who promptly whipped out the latest-model cell phone from his pocket and began texting while he conversed with Keith.

"Keith, my man. Do I sense some possessiveness for my Josie? I thought you were going to light me up for that hug." His fingers clicked madly over the tiny keyboard, his focus on the screen.

Jerk. If Josie wasn't counting on the guy as a client, Keith would bounce him out of the house right now.

He'd never had a real beef with him before, but now that he thought about it, Chase had always been kind of full of himself when he'd shown up at the Murphys' for a game of football or a weekend sailboat race. And now he was supposedly some big-deal investment banker.

Calling her "his" Josie?

Screw it. Keith didn't care if Josie wasn't fully on board with the plan to continue dating. He had just made it a high priority to convince her. He wanted her and he was staking his claim now, starting with this guy.

"And I thought she was a relative of yours." Keith dragged their bags inside the house and closed the front door. "Do you try to cop a feel with all your cousins?"

"Only the hot ones." Freeman took the opportunity to grin at him, looking up from his texting for the first time.

Bad. Mistake.

"About that." Keith yanked the phone out of the guy's hands and set it on the table near the door to be certain he had the idiot's full attention. "She's officially on the list of people you don't touch. Are we clear? I may be the most civil of my brothers, but not so much when it comes to her."

"Damn, man. You could have clued me in *before* you let me put my foot in my mouth." Chase held up his hands, surrendering the cause. "How was I to know you and Josie were an item?"

"She walked in here with me, didn't she?" Keith wondered how some people got through the day being so clueless.

Then again, he wondered where all the macho posturing came from on his part, since that wasn't usually his style.

He backed up a step, giving himself some space to cool off. At the same time, he heard a throat clear on the opposite side of the large, sunny family room that dominated the Murphy home beyond the foyer.

"Hope I'm not interrupting anything." Danny, Keith's younger brother and the next in birth order, sauntered toward them across a blue-and-white braided wool rug, a football under one arm. "Although I gotta say you two make a cute couple."

"At least I'm not bumming off my parents between Navy stints and tossing the pigskin in the backyard on a weekday like some teenage delinquent." Keith stretched his arms out at a right angle to his body, his forefingers and thumbs forming the tripod that was the universal receiver's stance to call for the ball.

Danny lifted his arm to fire a pass, putting some serious zip on the ball even though they were indoors and a wall of windows fanned out behind his brother.

Chase leaped behind Keith to back him up, apparently reluctant to see a window shatter. Fortunately, Keith had hands like glue, snagging the ball neatly out of the air even though he had to coax every extra millimeter out of his vertical leap to manage the feat. He didn't have time to savor the athletic victory, however, since Danny wasn't done firing bullets.

"The advantage of hanging out at the family home base is knowing better than to bring a new girlfriend around when an ex-girlfriend is due to arrive with Dad at any minute." Dan snagged a baseball cap from a high bookshelf and jammed it on backward as he stalked over to retrieve his ball. He paused near one of the tall windows he'd almost taken out a minute earlier. "In fact, I think that's Ray Blaylock and his daughter in the driveway with Dad now."

Ah, crap.

Keith hoped in vain that Dan was just messing with him. As he peered out the window, he could see his father had just emerged from his silver Mercedes as Ray—his occasional business partner—parked a sleek blue BMW behind him. Ray Blaylock owned a casino chain and had been working on Keith's father to open resorts near a handful of the Blaylock casinos.

A deal that didn't matter to Keith one way or another. Except that Ray was grooming his only child to take over the casino business one day. And that meant Keith's ex—the spoiled jet-setter, Brooke—was unfolding her long legs from the front seat of the Beamer even now.

UPSTAIRS, JOSIE FOLLOWED Keith's mother past another en suite bedroom—one of at least six she'd seen in the mammoth house, which had to be at least ten thousand square feet. But the sprawling seaside mansion wasn't just another spectacle built to parade a fat bottom line, the way many exclusive properties were. The Murphy home looked just like that—a home. And Josie had quickly realized the driving force behind the gracious warmth of the place was her elegant and amiable tour guide.

Any worry she'd had about meeting Keith's mom had dissipated after a conversation about ostrich feather fringe—a small thing that Josie had quickly picked up on after seeing the quirky detail in multiple rooms, used in a variety of ways. While the extra bedrooms—presumably rooms for her sons when they were living at home, or when they chose to return for visits—exhibited a decidedly male vibe, with strong colors and clean lines, the rest of the house came alive with sophisticated and romantic touches that were never overdone. An elaborate, imported chandelier hung over an antique bed that was deliberately shabby chic with a white cotton duvet. The ostrich-feather trim wavered on a nightstand lamp in the bedroom or wove through a pillow appliqué in the family area. A rescued mahogany bar in the game room stood comfortably beside a modern billiard table and a dartboard. An autographed black-and-white photo of a thirties' pinup girl featured a curvy blonde peeking mischievously over an ostrich-feather fan. Clearly, Colleen Murphy had managed to work in a nod to the feminine even in the most masculine of rooms.

Now, as Josie followed her hostess toward the east end of the house, she realized she'd rather spend the day enjoying the creative touches that made the Murphy home so charming than speak with Chase about his boat. How interesting to meet a woman who'd successfully navigated the same world of wealth that had led Josie's parents to a life of self-indulgence.

"It's my 'mom cave,'" Colleen Murphy confided as she led Josie into a spacious office with panoramic views of the Atlantic and the Monomoy Islands. "Of course, I decorated it before they called it that. But even ten years ago I knew this room would be just for me."

Josie sucked in a breath at the perfectly framed windows draped in layers of sheer curtains and peach-colored Italian silk. But more than the view was spectacular here—it was the manifestation of a beautiful space.

"You've got such an eye for design." Josie took in the prints of mandalas from all over the world on the wall opposite the windows, a kaleidoscope of color and pattern. The hardwood floor had been painted, cottage style, except for the stenciled words outlining the conversation area and the space around the antique writing desk. "There's so much to see in here. What is the stenciled message?"

Josie tried to follow the calligraphy, but wasn't sure where the words began.

"It's a mishmash," Colleen admitted, pointing to the various areas. "A little Walt Whitman. Some Gospel according to Matthew. And a long quote from the poet Rilke around the perimeter. They're mostly for me. Some people post affirmations on their mirror, but I wanted mine to be more permanent."

Affirmations?

Josie nearly did a double take to think this woman

with five hunky, successful sons—six if she counted the Finnish hockey player Keith had mentioned—needed affirmations of any kind. Colleen Murphy was married to a self-made man who'd pioneered a global resort conglomerate from humble beginnings as the owner of a clam shack on Cape Cod. But Josie tamped down her surprise. She, of all people, should know that just because a life appeared glamorous or well-adjusted on the outside didn't mean the inner life matched up. How long had Josie spent trying to distance herself from her family's ostentatious wealth, never comfortable with the life they chose to lead?

"'I celebrate myself, and sing myself,'" she read aloud, spotting the Whitman poem. The quote from Matthew looped around a stone fireplace tucked in the corner. "'From where your treasure is, there will your heart be also.' I can see where you'd enjoy reading those words every day."

Colleen moved closer to view the room—the mom cave that amounted to a highly personalized living space—from Josie's perspective.

"I never get tired of them." She tucked a stray lock of hair behind one ear, where a simple diamond stud glittered in the sunlight. "I used to like coming up here at night if Robert was still at work and the boys had tired me out during the day. It helped to remember my treasure was here, in this home, even though Keith had tried to gut a hundred-pound fish in my kitchen or Danny had used the chef's-grade knife sharpener on his hockey skates and nearly lost a finger in the process."

Josie laughed. "They must have been a handful."

"They still are," she murmured, leaning to peek out the bank of windows. "In fact, I see the potential for another Murphy gaffe in the driveway, and I wonder if you might do me a favor?"

Curious, Josie moved to join Colleen by the windows. "Don't tell me they went fishing while we were touring the house."

She couldn't imagine what kind of "gaffe" Colleen could foresee in the calming ocean view. Although, now that she looked closer to the house, Josie could see two cars that hadn't been in the driveway before.

What company could have arrived that would be any worse than Chase?

"Not exactly." Colleen stepped closer and dropped a manicured hand on Josie's arm. "Would you mind giving Keith the benefit of the doubt when you meet his ex-girlfriend?"

The words clarified the trouble brewing, even as they sent a surprise wave of dread through Josie. Not that she had exclusive rights to Keith. Far from it. They'd only just met and…

Who was she kidding? If she was honest about her feelings, she'd have to acknowledge a desire to seek out Keith and wrap herself around one arm like a tattoo, just so his ex knew she'd better back off. And didn't that knock Josie for a loop, to concede a staggering amount of jealousy where he was concerned? She needed time to retreat and think about where this was going before she did something impulsive and made a fool out of herself. Taking a deep breath, she struggled to remain gracious.

"I'm not sure what you mean." Plastering on a polite smile, she mentally armed herself to fake her way through meeting the ex without throttling a woman who'd hurt Keith once upon a time.

"I mean that Brooke Blaylock is a poor reflection of my son's taste in women." Colleen smoothed the drape she'd lifted to see out the window, restoring the room to perfect order before she headed for the door. "Will you keep that in mind and try not to hold it against him?"

Sighing, Josie knew that escape out the back door was no longer an option. She needed to be a grown-up in front of Keith and his family, and that meant suffering through a meeting with his ex. An ex who might very well recognize Josie from her fashion-designing days, when they'd no doubt run with the same crowd.

"I promise to be open-minded," she agreed. "If *you'll* let me come back and photograph this room as an inspiration piece for my studio. My assistant, Marlena— she's practically a partner in my firm—would love to see what you've done with this space."

"Deal." Colleen led her back toward the foyer, where voices and laughter echoed.

Josie braced for impact, hoping Keith's mother would remain as warm and welcoming if Josie's bad-girl past was revealed. Because despite the fact that Keith thought Josie and his ex were worlds apart, she couldn't help but fear her time of hardworking anonymity was about to implode.

10

So MUCH FOR the homecoming.

Keith stood in the family room, listening hard for the sound of Josie's voice. He'd find her. Intercept her. Spirit her out the back door. It wasn't exactly the way he'd wanted this visit to go down, but she wouldn't thank him if she had to meet his ex-girlfriend on her first visit to his family home. Either way, he'd mop the floor with his brother later if he found out that Danny could have given him an earlier heads-up on the Blaylocks' arrival.

As Keith caught the echo of his mother's laughter in the east wing, he headed up the stairs. Josie and his mom were just coming toward him, so he swooped in and hooked an arm around Josie's waist.

"We need to head out," he informed her before he leaned in to give his mother a kiss on the cheek. "The Blaylocks just pulled in and I don't think Josie deserves to be thrown in with the lions on her first visit."

"I'll be fine—" Josie began, as his mom's brow furrowed.

"Are you sure?" Colleen asked, while Keith tugged Josie toward a bedroom with a balcony that had stairs to the back lawn.

"Positive. Just have someone shove the luggage out onto the porch so I can grab it."

Josie halted on the carpet, digging in her heels. "Keith, I'm sure we can at least say hello. We don't need to run out the back door—"

"No worries," his mother assured her, smoothing a hand along Josie's forearm. "I do hope you'll come back soon?"

"I'd like that." She nodded and squeezed Colleen's hand. "Thank you so much."

Keith could feel the tension in her spine and knew she hated to run out of his house through a back bedroom. But then, she had no idea what she was up against. Brooke would make nice in front of his family, but she hadn't taken their breakup well and Keith wouldn't put it past her to cause trouble if she could. Better to get out now.

Steering Josie toward the French doors, he slid the screen open and ushered her through.

She paused once more, frowning. From downstairs, Keith could hear Brooke calling out greetings, her throaty tone unmistakable as it drifted up from the foyer.

Tugging Josie across the balcony and down the steps, he pointed her toward the front lawn, while he wondered

how he could make a quick getaway. A cab could take
a while. He ducked inside the garage to see what cars
were available and what he could get out of the driveway with the other vehicles parked there.

When he emerged, phone in hand to call a cab, after
all, Josie was already halfway down the driveway, her
determined steps sharp on the pavement. Damn it.
Didn't she realize he was only trying to help her dodge
a bullet?

"Josie." He called to her as his brother pulled up his
car—a classic Gran Torino he must have had stashed
by the tennis courts.

At least Danny had done something helpful. Now all
Keith needed was the luggage. He darted up the walk-
way to grab the bags from the porch, just in time to see
Brooke Blaylock stationed at one of the sidelights to the
front door, her attention focused on Josie.

The pinched frown on Brooke's face made him all
the more grateful he'd gotten Josie out of there. It had
been the perfect plan. Scooping up the bags, he followed
her, free and clear of any drama.

IF ANGER COULD HAVE fueled her trip back to Boston,
Josie would be there already.

As it was, she marched down the driveway, unwill-
ing to skulk around in the bushes with Keith while he
avoided his ex.

"Need a lift?" Keith's brother Danny called to her
from the window of a classic car she didn't recognize,
a burgundy-colored vehicle with a black hardtop.

He pulled up from out of nowhere, parking the vehicle at the end of the drive before hopping out. Behind her, she could hear footsteps and the wobbly roll of suitcase wheels across the pavers. No doubt Keith was on his way.

"How did you know I needed one?" She smiled gratefully at Danny, a slightly shorter, more muscular version of Keith—except that he hadn't had a haircut in months.

From the goatee and longish hair to the vintage American car and backward baseball cap, Danny Murphy didn't fit the mold for his wealthy, high-powered family.

"I saw the train wreck coming a mile away," he declared, his voice raised to make sure anyone else in the front yard could hear. Then, leaning closer, he lowered the volume for her ears alone. "If you can drive a stick, you can be halfway to Beantown before he catches you."

She had to admit the idea had a smidge of appeal, after being dragged out the back door, but she didn't trust herself driving the shiny, mint-condition Ford, which looked as if it had been waxed every Saturday since it rolled off the production line.

"Josie, wait." Keith's warm bass tone drifted on the breeze like her conscience talking to her.

Hazy memories of that same voice making sexy suggestions in her sleep stirred an unwanted response from her even now. Why did she find him so appealing when she was so irritated with him? But even when faced with a man every bit as handsome as Keith—and Danny

Murphy surely qualified—she still found herself longing for Keith's voice in her ear. His persuasive mouth on hers.

"He's gaining on you," Danny warned, his eyes on his brother while he goaded her. No, more likely he was goading Keith.

She thought about their mom, tucked away in her pretty room surrounded by her affirmations. No wonder Colleen Murphy needed them, if the rest of her sons were as confrontational as these two.

Turning, Josie spied Keith as he ditched the bags at the end of the walk. He spared a momentary murderous glance at his brother, but when his green eyes landed on her, she saw only concern. Worry.

"How kind of you to loan out the Torino on such short notice," he barked at his brother. "You could make yourself useful and load up the bags, since you seem to have found the afternoon so entertaining."

"That's okay," she protested, her frustration tough to maintain when she was surrounded by a veritable force field of male posturing. "I was just about to call a cab."

Fumbling for her cell phone, she was surprised to see Danny stalk across the driveway for the luggage. He hefted both Keith's bag and hers in his arms and carried them toward the trunk.

Josie scowled at Danny. "I thought you were on my side," she grumbled, giving up the fight to locate her cell phone. She needed to get back to Boston sooner or later, and she might as well settle things with Keith before she got home.

The maelstrom of feelings she'd experienced in the last twenty-four hours told her she was in over her head with him. She needed to regroup and rethink what she wanted in her life. Even if she wanted him—and a twinge of jealousy over his former relationship made it apparent that she did—she had to consider the consequences of seeing him.

He'd probably been wise to keep her away from an ex-girlfriend with an ax to grind. What if the woman made the connection between Josie's current work and her former gig in fashion? Brooke Blaylock—and, yes, Josie knew the family, thanks to her copious scouring of the society pages—was definitely someone who stalked fashion designers for free swag. What if she'd seen Josie back in the days she'd trolled New York clubs to promote her attempts at haute couture?

Danny dumped the bags in the trunk and shut it with the gentle touch of a man who respected his car. "Hey, I tried helping you, but you've gotta move quick to outrun a Murphy man. That's just the cold, hard truth."

"I'll keep that in mind." She reached out to shake his hand in thanks, but he lifted hers to his lips and kissed the back of her fingers like a courtier.

This time, he didn't seem to do it just to bug his brother. He met her gaze head-on, his green eyes a shade darker than Keith's and far more inscrutable.

"Good luck to you, Josie Passano." He relinquished her hand, striding back toward the house and leaving the car to them.

"It's only a few minutes to the marina," Keith told

her, his voice sounding as weary as she felt. "We can retrieve your car, and I hope you'll still allow me to drive
you back to Boston." He opened the passenger door for
her, holding it wide.

The sun was slanting westward, she noted. It had to
be almost five o'clock. Time to get back to reality. Her
unscheduled vacation was over.

"That's fine." She had taken refuge in her work all
her adult life and now would be no different. She would
tell Keith as much on the ride back. "It's not your fault
she showed up. You mentioned that your families do
business together."

Sliding into the car, Josie buckled her seat belt while
he came around to the driver's side and put the vehicle
in Reverse. She watched the Murphy home grow smaller
in the distance.

Josie had been there only briefly, but didn't like to
think she might never return. She'd enjoyed talking with
Colleen, a woman who'd invested so much of herself in
her home and family. While Josie hadn't pictured that
kind of life for herself—still couldn't—she admired
the way Keith's mom had made the design of a house a
gift of love to her family. Whether or not the men in her
life realized it, they were surrounded by her thoughtful
care for them night and day.

Josie had even liked Keith's brother—the rebel
prankster who'd provided a getaway car for her even
though they were practically strangers.

"You're fortunate to have such a great family," she
observed, surprised at the sudden frog in her throat.

Apparently vacations made her emotional, because she suddenly felt far too raw. Oddly vulnerable. She hadn't dwelled on her own family's shortcomings in years, preferring to put their selfish hedonism and colossal laziness out of her mind most of the time.

"Wow." Keith peered across the front seat at her before turning his eyes back to the serpentine streets that were taking them to the marina. "I've been bracing myself over here for you to be furious about sneaking out to avoid Brooke. I'm surprised you're taking away positive thoughts about my family in light of the ridiculous awkwardness of going out the back door the first time I bring you home."

"It's not your fault she showed up."

"Still." His thigh muscle flexed as he shifted gears. "I'm sorry—"

Josie reached across the car interior to close his mouth with one finger. "Don't. You have no need to apologize. And don't forget, I've been dealing with the Brookes of the world my whole life, so I probably could have held my own. Just the same, I don't blame you for not wanting to take the risk of her recognizing me."

Keith shook his head. "It's not that. I just didn't want you to have to deal with her on your first visit to my home. I've no doubt you could have handled her. Can I explain one thing and then we never have to talk about her again?"

"One thing," she agreed, seeing the marina ahead and anxious to put Brooke Blaylock behind them.

"Have you ever met someone who seemed one way

and then you realized they weren't the person you thought they were?"

Her stomach knotted and she hoped he wouldn't say the same thing about her one day. But damn it, she'd tried to tell him about her past.

"I'm a bit of a dating novice," she admitted. "Since college, I've been absurdly focused on work."

"Come on. No one's ever broken your heart?"

She bit back her instinctive response—a deflection that might have made him smile, but sure wouldn't have answered the question. And since he was being honest with her, she thought she'd try some truth in return.

"I'm really skilled at not letting people too close." She pointed out her hybrid SUV in the marina parking lot. "When I first began dating, I kept people at a distance because I didn't want to let anyone see my dysfunctional family. Later, I did it because it had become habit. The couple of guys I've dated for any length of time were as work oriented as me."

Keith tucked into a spot beside her vehicle and shoved Danny's keys over the visor. A set of dog tags that must have been tucked there fell out onto Keith's lap. He gathered them up and slid them into the console between the seats, next to a pool of change and guitar picks.

"Well, for me, love is blind, and I guess I haven't used good judgment a couple of times." He turned toward her in the seat. "With Brooke, I saw someone who was as active and outgoing as me. She liked getting out and meeting people, and so did I. After a while it became apparent that while I enjoyed impromptu football games and sailboat races, she preferred going to clubs and parties every night."

"When people want to impress someone they like, they can put on a good show." Josie had seen it happen plenty of times in the world she'd grown up in, where people air-kissed their worst enemy to maintain a facade. "I'm sure Brooke can be very dazzling when she wants to be."

Although Josie could imagine he would grow tired of someone who cared more about socializing than working toward a goal he or she was passionate about. Josie identified with that side of him—the tireless worker, building a business and an idea. And while she'd relished every second of their sensual encounters, she had also really enjoyed that first lunch together in Nantucket, when he'd told her about his company.

"Do you remember her?" he asked, opening his car door and withdrawing the luggage from the trunk, while Josie unlocked the SUV. "From back in the days where you worked in fashion?"

"No." She handed him the keys to her vehicle, only too glad to let him contend with the traffic on the way back to the city. "Because even though I went out to the clubs in New York all the time back then, I was ruthlessly focused on my career. She could have had a twenty-minute conversation with me, and unless she had something interesting to say about clothes or design, I guarantee I was either critiquing what she wore or else thinking about another piece for the collection I wanted to develop one day. I was that obsessed with work."

With the transfer of luggage complete, Keith fired up her SUV and adjusted the mirrors and seat to suit his larger frame—his powerful, perfectly made body that had turned her inside out more than once the night before. She swallowed the swell of hot desire, cracking her window to get some air.

"What made you leave a job so compelling?" he asked, swiveling in the seat to look out the rear window before he backed from the parking spot.

The million-dollar question. And it was past time she shared the details that made a future for them so difficult.

"A gossip columnist." No. That wasn't right. Hadn't she taken responsibility for that time in her life by now? "Actually, a gossip columnist who capitalized on my stupidity and my family's reputation."

Keith pulled out onto the main road heading off the Cape and toward the city, at ease behind the wheel even though he'd never driven her vehicle before. He didn't ask any questions, letting her talk at her own pace. Which was just as well, since the only thing to do was blurt it out.

"I chose to leave the fashion industry when a tabloid journalist snapped a picture of me kissing a guy in a back alley outside a club at closing time."

She peered over at Keith to gauge his reaction as they reached the intersection with Route 3N.

"No harm in that though, right?" He shrugged, seeming to sense there was more to the story.

"Except I didn't know he was married." Her work was high stress and she'd indulged in a kiss. It shouldn't have been the end of the world. Too bad the guy turned out to be a cheater and a liar.

"But if you didn't know—"

"Turned out I also didn't know he was a newly elected congressman who had ticked off the gossip columnist in question."

Keith's jaw flexed. Tightened. She suspected he was beginning to see the potential difficulty she would have establishing a relationship with anyone remotely in the public eye.

"Did that bastard politician ask you to leave your job to help him cover up a scandal?"

"No. He was in the wrong, so I let him fend for himself with the wife and the papers." She'd hung him out to dry, and she didn't think adultery went over any better in the Midwest than it did in the Big Apple.

Technically, she hadn't slept with him, but cheating was cheating, and back-alley kisses with married men never played well in the press.

"So why leave a job you loved?" He frowned. "I can't picture the fashion world being all that uptight about an occasional scandal."

"I left my job because *I* don't care for scandal, and the design world invites tabloid journalism. The misstep with the congressman wouldn't have been a big deal for someone else." Another aspiring designer would have gotten a second chance. "But my parents are always in the papers, and they've been in and out of rehab more times than I can count. There was too much material for future scandals, and I didn't care to remain in a world where I had to constantly look over my shoulder for fear of paparazzi trying to wreck my life."

11

KEITH SIFTED THROUGH Josie's revelations on the trip back to Boston, finally seeing the reasons for her reservations about dating someone like him. Back on the *Vesta,* when she'd told him about her party-girl past, he'd reacted poorly, but had dismissed the issue fairly easily, knowing that image of her didn't match the woman she was today. But now he could better appreciate the deeper problem.

It didn't matter that she didn't fit the mold of a pampered socialite princess with a love of the high life. The media liked that image of her. She was beautiful and bound to inherit a small fortune, even if she never willingly took another cent from her dissolute parents. The Davenport name was well known in New York circles— probably the reason she'd opted to try her design business under a new name in Boston. An attractive heiress with money to burn who had the slightest inclination for scandal was a perfect recipe to sell newspapers and guarantee click-throughs online. The truth of Josie Passano would never compete with the myth of Josie Davenport, fashion diva and home wrecker. The story was just too juicy.

And certain to cause more trouble for her down the road. He knew it, and he suspected she knew it, as well. If anything, a relationship with him—a young entrepreneur on the rise, from a family with some wealth in their own right—would only hasten renewed interest in her. And by extension, him. The timing wasn't great when he was eager to lock down the partnership with Wholesome Branding.

So how connected did he feel to this woman he'd known—and slept with—for the last two days? Two mind-blowingly incredible days. He didn't know where they could take things from here, but he wasn't ready to give her up.

"You can't run from the past forever," he observed as he wound through the South End toward the address on Harrison Street that she'd given him.

They passed rows of brownstones and a Venezuelan restaurant where the dinner crowd spilled out the door onto the street as they waited for tables. It was a vibrant neighborhood he hadn't driven through in a while. Young couples walked their dogs in front of a bakery advertising organic pet treats. The music from a tapas bar drifted on the breeze.

"I didn't run." She pointed out her building, a brownstone painted white and sandwiched between a tailor shop and a Chinese restaurant. "I turned away from it and didn't look back."

"But you changed your name." He parked the SUV on the street, wondering if he could find some way around her very public past if he dug deep enough. Searched hard enough.

He needed all the facts.

"The name change was actually long overdue," she said, hopping out of the vehicle at the same time as he did, not giving him a chance to open her door.

"Will you at least let me take your bag up for you?"

She hesitated, clearly uncertain about his expectations.

"I'll call for a cab to pick me up. I live by the river in Back Bay, so I'm not too far." He wanted to put her at ease. No pressure. No obligations. "I won't stay long if you don't want me to, but I'm curious to see your studio, since your work is such a part of you."

Nodding, she seemed to accept that statement at face value. And, of course, it was absolutely true. But if he saw any indication that she'd like him to stay…

Damn, but it had been too many hours since he'd had her in his bed. His hands ached to touch her, to wrap her up and pull her against him. Yeah, and if he continued on that train of thought, they'd never make it inside. Clearing his throat, he steered the conversation back to her run-in with the tabloid media.

"So you would have changed your name even if you hadn't left New York?"

He pulled her bag out of the hatch, the canvas stretched to the seams because of the sample books she'd packed. The scent of Chinese food from the restaurant next door steamed through the air as the sunset turned the sky purple.

"Yes. I tried using Passano as soon as I turned eighteen, but the design house I worked for preferred to slide in the Davenport name wherever possible. It was a conversation piece for them that the daughter of a well-known New York family worked there," she muttered darkly, unlocking the door to her building. She motioned him past a wall of mailboxes toward an ancient elevator in the small foyer.

While the building was hardly dilapidated, it was definitely old. Clearly, she hadn't followed her parents' lead in raiding the family trust fund to finance her work space. The Davenports owned a property on Central Park West, close to the upscale Manhattan hotel that had been in their family since the turn of the century. That kind of money would have bought Josie the best address in Boston if she'd cared to tap into it, and he couldn't help but admire her refusal to take the easy path.

"You were a scandal waiting to happen," he observed, following her into the old-fashioned lift.

"Exactly. I was on a collision course with disaster from the moment I set foot in a field soaked with gossip and fueled by name recognition." She inserted another key into the elevator control panel to send them up to the loft level, and they began a surprisingly smooth ascent. "I haven't given it much thought since I moved to Boston and left my fashion aspirations behind, but I'm pitching an interior design television show to a local cable network and I've been bracing myself for the issue to resurface."

She bit her lip as she stared at the needle on the wall pointing out the floors they passed. Coming to a slow stop, the elevator opened directly into the loft space. She flipped a switch before they entered a high-ceilinged artist's dream studio, illuminating the exposed brick walls and tall windows with night lighting. A low-level blue glow emanated from a handful of pendant lamps suspended over a massive fabric table in the center of a two-person work space. Two desks faced opposite sides, their respective views littered with bulletin boards and easels full of notes and drawings, color photographs and bits of fabric trim pinned at odd angles.

Beyond, Keith could see a client meeting area with love seats, and a wet bar with an espresso machine. And past that, an archway stenciled with a fairy-tale rose arbor seemed to indicate the transition to the loft's private space, where Josie's living quarters must be.

"Come on in." She dropped her purse on a table by the elevator door and left her shoes on a jute mat to one side of the entryway.

Toeing off his loafers, Keith followed her, absorbing her world as he took in the details of the place where she spent so much of her time. As he neared the rose arbor painting, he could see delicate fairies and hideous goblins hiding side by side in the greenery.

"Did you do the artwork?" he asked as she flipped on a light inside the kitchen on the other side of the archway, bringing the layout of the living quarters into focus.

The kitchen backed up to a dining area and living room. He'd guess the bedroom and any other space must be down a short hall around the far end of a bookcase near the television. As much as he hoped to make it to her bedroom tonight, he liked learning more about her, too.

"No. That was my assistant's birthday gift to me." Josie pulled glasses out of the cupboard and poured them each a seltzer.

"She must be very talented."

"You have no idea." Josie gestured toward the breakfast bar at one end of the small kitchen. Neat white cabinets occupied two walls, streamlined and modern. "I'm so fortunate to have her. She's been instrumental in helping me come up with a unique pitch for a television design program. We think that kind of exposure will really grow our business."

"How soon are you marketing the show?" He took the seat she'd pointed out—a bar stool tucked under the butcher-block countertop—determined to find a place for himself in her life.

"As soon as we have some photos from Chase's boat redesign." She leaned a hip against the sink and sipped her water. "Next month, I hope."

"So you'll need to come up with a plan to handle the inevitable buzz in the tabloids by then, right?" His eyes followed her feminine curves.

But if they could contain the fallout from her past, it would make a future a hell of a lot easier.

"With any luck. I have to admit I feel a lot more confident in my design abilities than my skills with media spin." She swirled the ice cubes in her glass.

"Would you consider help from the public relations department at Green Principles?" He had invested a significant part of the company budget in the marketing department early in the process of building his business. "I've assembled a solid team over the years. They could assist you in managing the release of information and—if necessary—administer damage control."

He could tell it hadn't been the right tactic when she met his gaze over the rim of her tumbler. There was a cool stillness in her eyes.

"Absolutely not." Straightening, she set her glass in the sink. "I've built my business from the ground up, with no help from the deep Davenport pockets. It's a fact I'm proud of, and I don't intend to give control away to anyone for the sake of making my job easier."

He put up his hands to halt the outpouring of strong emotion. "Wait. I think what I said must have came out wrong."

"This is something I feel very strongly about." She crossed her arms. Immovable.

"I see that. But would you just hear me out?"

He took her silence as a green light.

"You wouldn't be giving up anything. And it would be a direct benefit to me, since our business identities will be inevitably linked if we continue to see one another."

"No handouts," she asserted, shutting him down. "I'll handle any tabloid interest on my own. It's one thing to insist on paying for dinners. It's another altogether to suggest I use your company resources."

Her clipped words reminded him of how emphatic she'd been about not taking the sailboat voyage with him initially. But he'd talked her around to his way of thinking then, hadn't he? And she deserved some professional PR advice now even more than she'd needed a vacation from her seven-day workweek. Maybe if he set the argument aside for now, he could revisit it more successfully later.

"I understand." He carefully didn't agree or disagree, knowing he might need to call in the help eventually if she got in over her head with the tabloids. "I respect that you've built your business on your own."

Setting his empty glass on the counter, he came around the bar to confront her about where they stood now that their feet were on dry land. It had been too long since he'd touched her. Her eyes widened as he neared. He stopped inches from her, standing toe-to-toe with her on the blue wool throw rug that covered a polished hardwood floor.

"Thank you." She stared up at him with that steady gaze of hers. She wasn't an eyelash batter like Brooke. And he appreciated that when Josie played games, she brought him along for the ride. But she seemed serious now.

"So where do we go from here?" he asked, settling his hands on her waist. "I'm not ready for our time together to end."

She went still and he found himself holding his breath.

"I'm not, either," she admitted finally, the lapels of her blazer parting as she lifted her hands to rest on his chest. The clean scent of tea rose drifted up from her skin, light and delicate.

Thank You, God. Relief kicked through him with surprising force.

He moved to pull her closer, but she splayed her hands on his chest, not finished with their conversation.

"But maybe we should wait until you firm up your deal with Wholesome Branding and I lock down the television show."

He ground his teeth together, not liking that answer one bit. Releasing her, he turned away in frustration. His need for her had grown by the hour since they'd met. He hadn't realized the depth of that hunger until he'd seen her so-called cousin touching her. Residual possessiveness still burned his gut.

"And after those deals are closed, we'll have others lined up that we won't want to disrupt. As work-oriented as we both are, there will always be something important happening when it comes to our jobs."

"So what do you suggest?" She came up behind him, her fingers walking a path up his back.

Heat flared where she touched him and spurred a deeper burn where she didn't. He turned to face her.

"Maybe we can keep things quiet for a few weeks." He worked the buttons on the front of her blazer, needing to touch more of her. "Just between us."

"A secret affair?" She quirked a brow and he heard the teasing note in her voice.

"We can finish the vacation we didn't get to have on the *Vesta*. Long nights alone. Late dinners where I cook decadent things and feed you with my fingers." He reached up to stroke her lower lip. "You don't have to worry about who picks up the check because you'll be too busy thinking about me picking you up and carrying you to bed."

"Sounds tempting." She leaned closer, nipped his finger. "But I don't want to be the cause of you losing your deal. I know it could really expand Green Principles into global markets."

"I'm not going to lose anything." He'd pursued Wholesome Branding for too long. It was a win-win situation for both parties. "Whereas I've got everything in the world to gain."

He punctuated the statement with a kiss that left them both a little breathless.

"I'm sure they call themselves 'Wholesome' for a reason," she reminded him, her breasts grazing his chest.

"And nothing we do is going to take that away from them." He'd retreated from dating for too long, denying himself a basic human need.

Besides, Josie wasn't just a date. She was special. Sexy and smart, confident and ambitious. The total package. And he had no intention of letting her slip away just yet.

Slanting his mouth over hers, he took his powers of persuasion to the next level.

SHE'D NEVER INVITED a man here.

Not once in the two years since she'd bought the place. Her dates had been casual, her romantic life beyond reproach after the colossal mishap that had led to a tabloid frenzy. Now, Keith Murphy was crumbling defenses left and right, striding into her life and her space as if he belonged there. Making her forget all the great reasons she had for keeping guys at arm's length.

Trouble was, Keith wasn't just any guy.

And she was falling for him hard. Fast.

His kisses rained down her neck and over the neckline of the camisole she wore beneath her blazer. The jacket slid from her shoulders and off, an early casualty of his bold touch. She knew they were playing with fire to have an affair, even if they kept it out of the public eye. But Keith wasn't a married man and she wasn't cut from the same cloth as her pill-popping, martini-swilling parents. The tabloid media had scared her out of a career once. They wouldn't do it again, no matter the outcome of her time with Keith.

"Don't think about anything but this moment," he whispered in her ear, reading her mind as easily as he'd talked her into this crazy secret romance. He lifted his head from where he was raking the camisole strap down with his teeth. "Okay? Just us. Just this."

Right. She could do that. She wanted to do that. Keith was too amazing a man for her to approach this with anything less than her undivided attention.

"Got it." Rising on her toes, she brushed a kiss along his jaw, the scent of his aftershave like an aphrodisiac as it brought back vivid memories of other times they'd twined around one another. "But be forewarned that I plan to scour your ex-girlfriend from your brain tonight."

Arching her hips to his, Josie cradled his erection there. He throbbed against her, the hard length more than ready for freedom from his khakis.

"I wouldn't worry about—" He broke off midsentence when she slipped her fingers under the waistband of his pants and worked the fly open. "But if you insist…"

"Don't worry," she purred, kissing her way down his chest, his abs, until she knelt before him. "This won't hurt a bit."

She couldn't quite smother a smile when his eyes drifted closed at the brush of her fingertips along his shaft. She could feel the thick vein running the length of him right through his boxers.

Never before had it occurred to her to be so bold. But meeting Keith had unlocked deep, hidden hungers inside her. Now, it felt perfectly right to nuzzle him there with her cheek as she knelt on the woolen rug. To place a kiss on the tip before she slid his cotton boxers down and off.

His body was magnificently made and his sex proved

no different. He stood stiff and ready, his skin richly colored there. After skimming the taut shape with her hands, she wrapped her fingers around him and drew him to her lips.

The garbled sound he made marked the first and only time she'd rendered this smooth-talking man incoherent. Encouraged, she treated him with long, lingering swipes of her tongue, savoring the taste and texture. Humming in approval, she took him in her mouth, mimicking the squeeze of feminine muscles all around him. The animal growl in his throat was positively feral, thrilling her to her toes.

She liked this.

Too soon, he gripped her shoulders, dragging her to her feet. Dazed and ready for him, she pulled off her camisole and unfastened her bra while he worked on the fastening for her pants. His clever hands had her naked on the bottom half while she was still struggling with the lingerie straps, but he freed her of those, too, murmuring encouraging things in her ear as he walked her back toward the living-room couch.

She wanted to tell him she'd like to try new things, to take him to the pinnacle of desire with nothing more than her mouth. But words escaped her and she realized her whole body was trembling. Her skin felt as if electricity sizzled over every inch of her. Whatever she and Keith shared, it was powerful stuff.

Mute with hunger for him, she waited while he found a condom and sheathed his sex. A pity, since she'd been so ready to get more intimately acquainted with him.

But then he sat on the couch and drew her down on top of him, straddling him, and she forgot all about anything else she wanted.

When he entered her, the sense of completion rattled her to her core. It was a homecoming worthy of a drum solo and a parade, yet they'd been together this way less than twenty-four hours earlier. Every time they touched, the pleasure magnified and multiplied, until there was nothing else in her thoughts but him.

Winding her legs tight around him, she held him close. She never wanted to let him go.

Her body wept for him, all around him, making each thrust more lush and sweet than the last. She plunged her fingers into his hair and held him fast, kissing him thoroughly. All the while he steadied her and steered her, guiding her hips to where she needed to be. She was so glad someone had control, because she'd lost hers. Her brain spun somewhere in the stratosphere while her body blissed out on pleasure unlike anything she'd ever suspected she could feel....

The release catapulted her higher, launching a chain reaction of long, sweet spasms. She sank her nails into his shoulders, desperate for an anchor in a world gone hot and liquid. Keening cries startled her until she realized they came from her own throat. As the waves of pleasure slowed, he held her closer, burying himself deep inside her. She could tell he was nearing his own release, so she leaned back on his knees, increasing the contact and taking him deeper still.

The fierceness of his shout was every bit as primal as

hers had been, the low bass a vibration she felt against her chest.

As they gazed into each other's eyes afterward, Josie knew it was obvious to both of them that they'd crossed a boundary. They'd taken refuge in work to avoid their messy relationships—hers with her parents, his with a woman who'd let him down. But they couldn't hide from this, an attraction that had spiraled out of control.

"It's going to work out," Keith whispered in her ear as he wrapped her in his arms and drew her down to lie beside him on the couch. "You'll see."

12

"So you're dating Keith Murphy?" Marlena asked the next day as they sat across the studio's work island from each other, ostensibly brainstorming design possibilities for Chase Freeman's sailboat.

Josie's assistant had arrived at work before Keith left in the morning. If Marlena hadn't taken her increased responsibilities at the firm so seriously in Josie's absence, she probably wouldn't have come in so darn early, and Josie wouldn't be facing these uncomfortable questions. But as luck would have it, Keith hadn't quite made it out of the building. Their goodbye kiss near the elevator had been long and lingering, and they'd both been thinking about the next time they'd see each other, when the doors had opened and Marlena had emerged.

Hello, awkward.

During a hurried goodbye, Josie had agreed to go to his place tonight, as eager to check out his home as he'd been to see hers. Now, she debated how much to tell Marlena. While she trusted her assistant and good friend implicitly, Josie was still savoring the knowledge that she had an honest-to-goodness boyfriend. Apparently she'd reverted to middle school, excited about the fact that a guy actually liked her. But she wasn't ready to click the In a Relationship button on Facebook. Not with so much potential for controversy.

"Yes. But that's just between you and me." She flipped through a boating magazine for inspiration, then realized how it sounded to keep her relationship secret. "It's not like he's got another girlfriend or he's married or anything, though," she clarified.

Although after the scandal of three years ago, she would have understood if Marlena was concerned.

"I know he's not married," her friend groaned, her blue eyes alight with mischief. Two piercings lifted as she raised her left eyebrow. "He's one of the city's most eligible bachelors, so they seem to keep track of his dating status in the local society column. Actually, the gossip columnist keeps tabs on all the Murphy men. Did you know the oldest is getting married next spring?"

"Don't tell me you pay attention to the tabloid news." Josie flipped the pages of her magazine faster, not really seeing the boat interiors as her gut clenched in foreboding.

"I thought we agreed it was good for business to know who's who in this town?" Marlena frowned as she sorted through a box of ribbon trim on their worktable.

A shred violinist played in the background, some heavy metal performer that made Marlena swoon.

"We did." Josie sighed, distracted and worried all over again. "I'm just a little uneasy dating someone with that kind of prominent profile."

"Well, he's hotness personified. You should worry less about the consequences and more about enjoying yourself." Marlena reached into one of the cubbies under the table and shoved a handful of trim samples into her jacket pocket, preparing for her trip down to Chatham to look over the sailboat and begin working.

"That's the plan." Josie paused at an advertisement for her old design house's clothing line from last winter—a preppy-themed collection of resort wear. "Oh, this is perfect." She turned the magazine toward Marlena to show her the picture. "We should do Chase's boat in plaid and white—very sixties' country club."

"You know him better than I do. That picture makes me think of Mr. Howell from *Gilligan's Island*."

"That's him! Only thirty years younger." Properly inspired, she went to her swatch wall and started pulling out samples. "I still can't believe he signed that contract without a second thought."

"You're a fantastic designer," Marlena argued. "He would have been thickheaded not to."

"I think Chase would be perfect for Keith's ex-girlfriend," Josie mused, thinking how nice it would be to kill two birds with one stone—keep Chase out of her hair while she decorated, and keep Brooke well away from Keith.

"Brooke Blaylock?" Marlena filled a briefcase with

drawing supplies, her laptop and several product catalogs.

"Yes. You really do keep up to date on the society news, don't you?" She'd been so busy hiding from her own detestable brand of notoriety that she hadn't really considered how well known the Murphy name was around Boston.

Interest in Josie's romance with Keith would be high if it was discovered. And the consequences would affect more than Keith and his Green Principles business. How would it impact Murphy Resorts? Or Keith's soon-to-be sister-in-law who was trying to plan a spring wedding? A scandal could overshadow those happy plans.

Trepidation cooled some of the feel-good vibes that had fueled Josie's morning after a quickie in the shower with Keith. She could grow addicted to his touch.

"Possibly I take an interest in the local gossip for reasons beyond the professional." Marlena winked at her, the long, navy blue glue-on lashes fluttering over her cheekbone. "And as a tabloid fan from way back, I can tell you that the inevitable reprise of your congressman scandal is not going to hurt the company. If anything, we'll field a lot of calls from readers who want to meet you in person. But I predict that a lot of those curious callers will clamor for the right to say you designed their house."

Trepidation turned to all-out hives as Josie began to itch at the thought. "But I don't want to get business because of some dumb scandal." She scrunched up a handful of madras and tossed it across the table. "I want clients to come to me because of my work."

"Even if they hear about you through the tabloids, that doesn't mean they'd settle for inferior design results. No matter your reputation, you're only going to secure contracts through the merit of your decorating." Marlena retrieved the madras and smoothed the folds. "But if you're determined to hide a great guy from the world and smuggle him in and out of your office like a leper, that's your business."

Strapping her purple leather case closed, she whipped out her PDA and began clicking buttons.

"I'm not sure that's fair," Josie argued, hoping she hadn't made Keith feel like a fugitive this morning. "We agreed that—"

"Oh, crap." Marlena sank onto a bar stool next to the fabric table, her face pale as she stared at the screen of her BlackBerry.

"What?" Josie stilled, trying to read her friend. "Is everything okay?"

Marlena shook her head. "Have you turned on your phone yet?"

"No!" She jumped to her feet, hating that she'd forgotten, since her cell served as her business line. She hadn't even bothered to get a landline, for the sake of keeping costs down. "Sorry about that. Did we miss an important call?"

Retrieving her touch-screen device from the kitchen, where it had remained in her purse all night, Josie waited for the features to load.

"Not exactly." Marlena's voice hit a thin note and she had to clear her throat as she passed her own phone over to Josie.

The blog that filled the screen wasn't a missed call. But the headline in bold font proclaimed Manhattan Man-eater Targets Local Quarry. The headline came from a blog called Dishing It Up with Gloria, and the story featured an old picture from Josie's fashion-designing days next to a publicity photo of the congressman whose career had gone up in flames thanks to their scandalous kiss. Scrolling through text she only partly scanned, Josie found another picture—a grainy affair that must have been taken with a cell phone, but that showed her clearly enough. Sandwiched between Keith and Danny Murphy, Josie held her hand out to Dan as he kissed her knuckles. Behind her, Keith appeared ready to spit nails while Josie peered back at him.

To the casual observer, she looked as if she was deliberately baiting one guy with the other. The truth was her eyes had found Keith's because...he was important to her. She cared about him. A lot.

But only Josie knew that. To the rest of the world, she appeared every inch the simpering diva. And only one person could have captured the scene from this angle, from the Murphy house.

Brooke.

"Josie?" Marlena stood close to her, draping a comforting arm over her shoulder. "Are you okay?

"Maybe no one reads Dishing It Up with Gloria," she murmured, mindlessly handing back Marlena's phone and retrieving her own. Her fingers were unsteady as she worked the buttons, trying to review her messages for herself.

"I've got at least twenty tweets in the past ten minutes," Marlena said. BlackBerry back in hand, she scrolled through her digital world while the shred violin music continued to blast through the studio. "The Facebook messages are clogging my inbox and I'm getting texts every minute."

Shaking from the inside out, Josie scanned her email and found at least a hundred new messages in the past hour. From friends, strangers, *clients...* Questions like "Is it true?" and "Why did you change your name?" accounted for a lot of the headers, while furious rants about the evils of home wrecking accounted for more than a few. Several appeared to beseech her not to go near any of the Murphy men, bachelors who were apparently too good for her.

She wasn't sure how long she stood there, barely absorbing the tumult of words shaping her life, before she became aware of Marlena's voice beside her.

"Looks like the story originated on Gloria's blog an hour ago and it's already been picked up on *East Coast Fashion, Boston Design Time, Getting Juicy with Jillian*—"

"Oh, my God." Josie's knees didn't feel if they could hold her up, and she clutched the table for support before she sank gracelessly onto a stool at the island work space. "We only just got back into town yesterday."

Her heart beat wildly, nerves making her twitchy. "The whole world knows I'm dating Keith."

Worse, they were all rooting for him to dump her sorry butt, since she was a notorious party girl who ran with a wild crowd and spent her inheritance faster than she could hold her hand out for more. It didn't matter that the story bore no resemblance to her or her life. As Keith had predicted, the myth was more interesting than the fact.

Keith.

Did he know yet? He had to. She scanned through her messages and didn't see any from him. The thought of him being caught up in this kind of low-class gossip and cheesy scandal made her chest ache. She'd never meant to bring her past to his door. Damn it, she'd tried hard to avoid it.

But he'd been so persuasive, drawing her into his world and making her remember there was more to life than hard work and professional achievement.

Had he cut and run now that he'd seen what it was like to be at the center of sordid speculation and rumor? Frankly, she wouldn't blame him. Still, she double-checked the list of incoming messages, making sure she hadn't missed one from Keith. Hard to believe he wouldn't phone her after everything they'd shared.

Her phone rang constantly until she turned the volume off, not recognizing any of the names and numbers that came up on caller ID. None of them were Keith.

With her heart feeling more hollow by the moment,

Josie finally switched the phone off altogether. She couldn't think with the distraction of all those messages, when she wasn't even sure what she wanted to do yet. And the one man she needed to speak to hadn't bothered to call. Or text. Or contact her any other way. She was sure she understood why. That didn't make it any easier to accept, however, that there was a very real chance she could be on her own to ride out this storm. And unlike the last one, there was no safe harbor in sight.

KEITH'S OFFICE WAS a madhouse when he arrived. He'd discovered the exposé while he was in the cab on the way into work, at Green Principles headquarters in downtown Boston. He'd immediately tried to phone Josie, but the call had gone straight to voice mail. After a couple more tries, he'd put his efforts into damage control, knowing he'd need a good spin on the incident to salvage any chance of courting Wholesome Branding.

Damn it, he'd really wanted to expand his business overseas with them. But he'd be shocked if that could happen now. He wanted to ensure he didn't lose any existing clients over this new image of himself in the media. Because no matter what he'd told Josie, no guy wanted to be perceived as a boy toy for a spoiled socialite. And he had no illusions about the role he filled in this particular story line. He was the boy toy.

Now, locked behind his office doors with his marketing team, Keith tried Josie again. This time, his call went to voice mail faster than ever. Suggesting she'd turned the phone off? He certainly understood if she'd been trying to limit her calls, but how would he get in touch with her now? He'd have to find an email address for her and come up with a plan to handle this.

"Keith?" Rick, the public relations manager, was talking to him. Stylus gripped tight in one hand, he made notes on a laptop screen. "We'd like to issue a statement that you're not involved with this woman and that your acquaintance was brief and meaningless. We'll emphasize that you're the one who ended it—"

"No." Keith shook his head, sorry he hadn't interrupted the guy sooner. He'd worked with the same marketing group since the inception of Green Principles and they'd been dead-on plenty of times. But right now, they were way off. "Josie and I are dating and will continue to see each other. I don't need help lying to the press. I need help promoting my version of the story."

The PR manager—who had a real feel for the growing green market—appeared flummoxed. His yellow-and-blue-striped tie was already loose around his collar and it wasn't even noon. His sandy eyebrows furrowed in confusion.

"Date all you want." Rick threw open his arms expansively, as if to suggest Keith could hit on women far and wide for all he cared. "But we need to deny *this* relationship until we lock up the Wholesome Branding account."

"*We* need to?"

"It's our professional opinion—"

"Your professional opinion doesn't belong in my personal life. End of story." Frustration simmered, but the conversation made Keith appreciate that this situation might be trickier to navigate than what he'd originally guessed. "Josie Passano—and I want you to be consistent in calling her by that name only—is a very special woman in my life, and no manufactured tales about her are going to keep me away from someone I care about."

The room went quiet. Five guys and two women on the team stared back at him in silence from their seats around a small conference table. Behind them, a view of Boston Harbor filled the windows of their perch high above the city's financial district.

"Even if it costs you a substantial amount of business?"

One of the women posed the question or he might have thought the voice emanated from the depths of his subconscious, it so perfectly mirrored his self-serving ego—the ambitious part of him that had propelled his small business to this height.

Was he willing to give up the success that had bought him a Beacon Hill address before the age of thirty? Could he afford this kind of hit on a rapidly expanding business that not only improved the global environment, but had also won him some measure of acceptance from a notoriously difficult to impress father?

Damn it. Keith should have addressed the tough questions last night with Josie instead of letting the moment wash over him like a hot riptide. He'd gladly put aside the larger issues for the sake of passion, thinking they'd have more time to prepare for the potential obstacles before they arose.

Thanks to Brooke, that was no longer an option. And didn't that change the whole complexion of the issue? Perhaps the old rules no longer applied. Josie hadn't wanted any interference from his press staff. But he'd been blindsided, put in an untenable position—as had she. What choice did he have?

"Sir?" someone at the table prompted, while the guy closest to him shifted in his seat. "Should we proceed with our ideas or—"

"No." Keith needed to act fast. Trust his gut. Make the hard call that Josie wasn't ready to confront. "We're going to mount a large-scale media offensive and we need it by the end of the day."

With any luck, he would reach her before his counterstory hit the press. Because—no doubt about it—she wouldn't be happy to hear what he had in mind. He just prayed he could scrounge up enough persuasive skills to show her he'd chosen the only viable option. The only strategy he could think of that had a chance of saving both their businesses—and a chance at a future together.

13

JOSIE STARED AT THE street below her building, knowing she couldn't possibly escape without being seen by the media hounds clustered in a pack out front, hungrily waiting to pounce.

Marlena had left for Chatham to work on Chase's boat before the earliest of the gossipmongers had arrived, but by midafternoon there was a definite crowd. At first, Josie had thought the few folks milling around her stoop were just taking a smoke break from one of the local stores. Now, there could be no denying the group waited for her.

Anger burned through her veins. She hadn't gotten any work done all day, distracted and furious by turns that she was back in the same hot water that had turned her life upside down three years earlier. Maybe Keith was right that running wasn't a good response. But it had bought her enough time that she'd hoped the story would have faded from public interest.

She resented the feeling of being a prisoner here.

There was no hope of seeing Keith tonight at his place—he wouldn't want to see her now. He was probably busy trying to save his growing business from this debacle.

What would the media nightmare do to his company? Guilt twisted in her chest. She knew how hard he'd worked to achieve success that was separate from his family's fortune, and she admired him for that. If it hadn't been for her, if she hadn't stumbled onto the wrong sailboat in the first place, none of this would be happening. Of course, then she never would have met him, either, and she found that a whole lot tougher to regret.

Above her desk, the intercom from the downstairs lobby buzzed, its ring distinctive from the chime made by the one outside the building. Had a camera-wielding vulture managed to enter the lobby? She had very few neighbors, and to her knowledge, none of them had ever let strangers inside.

Tentatively, she went over to the intercom and pressed Talk, just in case it was some kind of legitimate business—a package delivery, maybe.

"Chinese for dinner," said a recognizable male voice that had filled her dreams. "Can you get me up there on the elevator?"

Keith.

A thrill went through her to think he'd gotten inside and was on his way to wait out a different kind of storm with her. At least, she hoped that's why he'd arrived.

"Absolutely." She pressed a button that would clear

the lift all the way to the top floor. "Hop in and make sure you're alone."

Anticipation made it the longest thirty-second wait of her life. What if he was upset with her? For all she knew, he could be furious about the scandal and ready to break off with her completely. She hadn't been able to gauge his tone over the intercom.

When the elevator door opened, he stood there holding a huge bag of food labeled with the name of the Chinese restaurant next door. The temptation to fling herself into his arms was too much to resist, so she didn't try. She ran at him as he walked into the loft, sliding her hands beneath his suit jacket to hug his waist. With her head tipped into his chest, she knew her first moment's peace since he'd walked out of the studio that morning.

"Remind me to bring you dinner more often." Kissing the top of her head, he leaned to set the food on the table in the entryway. "Who knew Chinese food would go over so well?"

He wrapped his arms around her, and she felt her heart rate slow, her breathing steady. Who knew she would become addicted to his touch—to him—in such a short time?

"I can't believe you made it in here without anyone noticing." Tensing, she edged back to peer up at him. "At least, I didn't hear any commotion outside."

"No one saw me," he assured her, smoothing her hair with a broad palm, his green eyes a safe harbor. "I went through the back entrance of the Chinese restaurant and told them I was picking up the usual dinner order for your studio."

She grinned. "Marlena and I have been known to order in a few times when we're working late."

"They handed me a bag a few minutes later, and the delivery kid knew how to access your second floor from their fire escape. After that, I just took the stairs down to the lobby to beg access to the penthouse suite, and here I am."

Her smile faded as new security worries cropped up. "I'm surprised they would be so quick to help you find your way in here. What if one of the bloodsucking reporters tries the same thing?"

"First of all, they're watching news coverage from Beijing in the restaurant, so I don't think anyone over there is aware you're a media star today." He plucked the bag up again and steered her toward the living area in the back. "Second, I gave the delivery kid a tip to offer egg rolls at a discount to the throng in front of your building, so I think they're going to make a killing off you. And I may have slipped him a few bucks to ensure he doesn't show anyone else the way he showed me. But even so, no one's getting up here on the elevator unless you want them to."

She followed him into her dining room off the kitchen and unpacked the takeout containers.

"Devious and brilliant all at the same time." She handed him the fried rice and grilled chicken that Marlena always ordered. "So what do you think of this mess we're in? I worried all day that you were going to put as much distance between yourself and this chaos as possible. For which, by the way, I would not have blamed you."

He sat, but didn't open the cartons of food, his hands folded on the glass-topped table she'd picked up at a salvage sale after a local furniture company flooded.

"That's not my M.O.," he reminded her quietly as she seated herself, his gaze steady. "And I would've liked to have been able to reassure you on that score, but I couldn't reach you all day."

His tone was perfectly reasonable. And yet something in it—or maybe in his stillness—gave her pause.

"I couldn't begin to formulate a response to all the calls and messages." Starving, she dipped a spoon into the steaming container of wonton soup and let the broth cool. "I just decided to shut things down and unplug until I can figure out my next move. I tried to call soon after you left—"

"I probably hadn't turned my phone on yet." He threaded his fingers together, his silk tie falling perfectly straight down his crisp cotton shirt despite a trip over a fire escape rail and through a second story window. "I wasn't ready for my vacation to end."

Memories of making love in the shower this morning and their heartfelt goodbye kiss returned with a vengeance. Warmth rushed through her in a way that didn't have a damn thing to do with wonton soup.

"Believe me, I'm sorry we had to come back early, too. If we were sailing down to Charleston on the *Vesta* right now, none of this would have happened."

They could be undressing each other in candlelight and playing sexy pirate games.

"But it did and we need to talk about where to go from here." Inside his jacket pocket, his phone buzzed. He pulled the phone out, studying the screen for a moment before dropping the device back into his pocket.

She'd set aside those reminders of the outside world all day, but now that Keith was here, it seemed she couldn't disregard the truth of the scandal any longer.

"I know my method of dealing with this isn't what you would have chosen—"

"What method of dealing with it?" he inquired, lifting a dark brow. "You've shut off connections with the outside world and locked yourself in a virtual tower, complete with goblins and fairies. To say that's living in a fantasyland wouldn't be off the mark."

Okay, that hurt. She blinked in surprise that he could deliver such a blow while seated before her so calmly.

"You're angry," she stated, trying to get a bead on the situation that she'd apparently misread. "When you arrived bearing dinner, I just assumed…"

Her cheeks heated and she cursed the emotions that bubbled up and made her too damn easy to read.

"Josie, I've been dying to see you—even just to talk to you—all day." The words seemed warm. Caring. But she knew anger and judgment lurked beneath them. "It's been a wrenching, hard-as-hell marathon at the office, and it sucked even worse that I couldn't touch base with you to know how you were doing during all this."

"I'm fine," she asserted with perhaps a bit too much force. Belatedly, she realized she'd said it through gritted teeth. Taking a deep breath, she tried again. "Perhaps I'm not fine at the moment, but I will be. I'll figure out what to do about this situation. I just needed some time to gather my thoughts—"

"And what happens in the meantime? The stories grow more tawdry because the tabloid media is forced to speculate, and you don't come to your own defense?"

"Wouldn't it be worse to say the wrong thing?"

"Which is why I wanted to lend you a hand in crafting the right statement—"

She made the time-out sign to cut off that line of thinking.

"Keith, this will never work if you view me as someone you need to bail out of trouble, someone to rescue, someone to—"

"Help?" he offered. "Josie, that's what people who care about each other *do.* They help one another. It's no different than when you took over the helm on the *Vesta* because I couldn't put out the storm sails and steer at the same time."

"It is different." Too restless to sit across a table from him and have this conversation in a reasonable, rational tone, she paced the dining room. "That's a case of lending an actual, literal *hand.* You're talking about bailing me out with resources well beyond my means, and I'm not going to live up to the media image of me as the pampered socialite princess who holds her hand out and assumes money will solve all her problems."

"So you'd rather close yourself off from the world and wait for the problems to go away on their own?" He stood, trying to intercept her in her pacing, but his phone went off again, distracting him.

"Yes," she retorted fiercely, pointing to his buzzing, vibrating pocket. "And that's why. We can't even have a conversation without the past intruding every two minutes. What's the sense of getting updates on a crisis when you don't know how to handle it or where to turn next?"

Her chest tightened as she thought about what this scandal could cost her. She'd been semisuccessful in shoving the worry aside all day, but now, with Keith here forcing the issue, she felt as if she was going to hyperventilate from the stress of it.

"I do know how to handle it," he assured her, that confident voice of his winding past her defenses and soothing her like the stroke of a hand.

"Is that so?" She wanted to believe he had a great idea for a way out of this mess, but his grim expression didn't give her much hope.

"I didn't have the option of turning off the phones at my office today. It was imperative I come up with a plan, and without your input, I was forced to develop a strategy that I thought would work best for both of us."

She frowned. "You didn't need to worry about me—"

"We are irrevocably tied in the media, so whatever I did was bound to have an effect on you. You have to see that." His voice was cool and distant and it made her anxiety spike.

Her neck itched.

"What are you saying?" she asked softly, wondering if it had been a mistake to not watch the news all day.

"I issued a statement to the media on our behalf." He withdrew a sheet of folded paper from his jacket pocket and laid it on the glass tabletop.

Her eyes flashed to his. "You knew I did not want you to intervene on my—"

"It says we've been quietly dating for months," Keith continued. "That shouldn't be a conflict for you, since you weren't dating anyone else during that time."

Confused, she couldn't understand why telling people they'd dated for months would help their situation. She watched in silence as he reached in his jacket pocket again.

And came out with a ring?

"The statement also went on to say we're engaged." Keith plunked a one-karat diamond on the table, his expression grim. "Congratulations, Josie. All of Boston is thrilled for us."

IF LOOKS COULD KILL, Keith imagined he'd be strung up from the loft rafters, swinging on a pendant lamp.

Or maybe she would have used two hands to push him out the window so he could land amid the "blood-sucking" reporters. Either way, Josie's dark eyes didn't convey any kind of relief, humor or—heaven forbid—joy to think of herself as his fiancée.

But instead of tossing the wonton soup in his face,

she backed up an unsteady step and sank heavily onto her chair.

"What have you done?" She blinked up at him, the anger fading from her eyes as quickly as it had arrived.

"Damage control," he asserted, refusing to feel guilty about it. "Josie, you don't have to back up the story if you don't want to. Or you can claim you returned the ring after the media spotlight was too much for the relationship. But if you wear the ring around town for a month, what's it going to hurt?"

"I didn't want you to do this." She stared at the princess-cut diamond as if it were a vial of snake venom. "You might not have known how I felt about the scandal when it broke, but we talked about the chances—"

"Someone needed to take action."

"So you twisted something special into a sham?" Her voice sounded close to breaking, and he wondered if he'd read her wrong. Was she mad?

Or hurt?

He settled into the chair across from her again, figuring the only thing he could do now was try to justify his position.

"It's not a sham. It's protection for you—for both of us—from a lot of sordid innuendo. If you wear this, interest in the congressman scandal will vanish. This is a new story." He shoved the ring closer to her, demanding she acknowledge it. "A *different* story. And a broken engagement isn't half as salacious as a politician sneaking around with a sexy heiress."

Finally, she picked up the ring, her hands trembling

just a little. From anger? Frustration? He knew she hadn't wanted him to take charge with the media, and he'd done so anyway. But what choice had she given him?

"Is this what it takes to save the Wholesome Branding deal?" she finally asked, turning the ring this way and that.

"I don't know if this will salvage it, but I can promise you that wasn't my main goal."

"No?" She ran a finger over the diamonds that circled the band. "But it was one of the goals."

"No, damn it." He wished she knew him better than that, but maybe their time together hadn't given her the same faith in him that he already felt in her. "I wanted to protect your business, my business and a relationship that I feel really good about, and not necessarily in that order."

"I appreciate what you tried to do." She set the ring on the table and lifted her gaze to meet his. "But I can't wear a lie. You were right that I can't keep running from this mess, but I'm not sure how to handle it yet."

The certainty in her dark eyes drilled a hollow place in his chest.

"So fine. We'll say you gave the ring back after the tabloid interest became too intense, and it drove us apart." That sounded reasonable in theory, a cover story his publicity team had fed him this afternoon when they were trying to cover all the bases.

But, in fact, it felt like crap.

She nodded, agreeing too damn easily.

Jamming the diamond back in his jacket pocket, he ground his teeth together. "Where does that leave us?" he muttered darkly, sensing a rift between them that he wasn't even sure he understood.

"I don't know." She shook her head, her dark hair grazing her shoulders in a silky sweep. "Things were complicated enough and I hadn't even processed the first part of the scandal. With this new development, it's a lot to digest."

She'd refused his plan. Refused the ring. Why would he think she'd want to forget all their problems in a make-out session in the kitchen? Frustration flooded his veins, but didn't begin to clear out the regret.

"You need more time," he guessed, unable to halt the hint of sarcasm that crept into his voice. But it was tough not to act out when she'd as good as kicked him to the curb.

"I guess I do," she admitted quietly, nodding.

"We set a new record for celebrity engagements." Standing, he recognized that she wanted him gone. "I blinked and it was over."

14

SITTING ALONE AT THE TABLE, Josie listened to Keith's footsteps as he retreated from her living quarters and headed toward the elevator.

A sexy, fantastic guy had proposed to her with the most beautiful ring ever. But while the rock had been real, the sentiment behind it had all been fake, and he'd done it only out of a need to save her from herself.

The knowledge that Keith saw her that way—as the maiden who locked herself in the tower and needed to be saved—rocked her. She'd always seen herself as strong, successful, ambitious. She plowed through life on her own terms, heedless of the resources her parents wanted to throw her way, refusing to accept aid from people who just wanted her to be a glittering reflection of themselves.

Had she missed the boat today by hiding her head in the sand? Heaven knew she had no idea what a healthy relationship looked like. Her parents' marriage was—

had always been—completely dysfunctional. What if she'd failed to recognize a true partnership?

She took her phone from the kitchen counter, determined to bring herself up to date on the sordid details of her life, wishing all the while that things hadn't gone horribly wrong with Keith, so they could sort through their email together. Commiserate over a common problem.

Make love until she couldn't see straight.

Her heart hurt at the thought that he was gone and wouldn't come back. But why had he astonished her with that incredible, gorgeous symbol of undying love, tossing it on the table as if it were a handful of nickels and calling it "damage control"? She might be a modern, independent woman, but she possessed enough estrogen to feel the romantic pull of an engagement ring, especially in the hands of her dream man.

Hadn't Marlena said all the Murphy males were on the tabloids' Most Eligible Bachelor lists? Josie would need ice in her veins to not be wooed by a ring from Keith. He, on the other hand, had made it abundantly clear the jewelry was a business proposition. A means to an end that would tidy up a PR mess of her own making.

The more she thought about it, the angrier she became. No, scratch that. Indignant was how she felt. Slamming down the phone, which was taking forever to load, thanks to the bazillion messages it surely contained, Josie stood and marched through her living quarters toward her work space.

She hadn't heard the chime for the elevator yet.

Maybe she could still catch Keith and give him a piece of her mind. Tell him all the reasons she hadn't needed saving and...

Her determined march into the work area stopped when she caught sight of him.

He stood by the wall of windows that overlooked the street, his dark head tipped down. He hadn't left. Her heart did a quick flip at the sight of him and hope fluttered in her stomach. At first she thought maybe he was staring at media below. And who could blame him for a moment's trepidation about venturing out into a mob like that? But when his elbow shifted, she realized he was looking at something in his hand.

The ring.

Softness curled inside her, putting out the fire that had been burning through her a moment before. She was about to clear her throat to let him know she'd entered the room when he suddenly turned his clear green eyes on her.

"Do you know I drew this ring on a Post-it note at lunchtime today and had one of my staffers go out and buy the closest thing she could find? I would have gone myself, but I was afraid if the press caught sight of me picking out the ring, you would hear about it before I could get here." He held it up in the slanting light, letting the reddish-gold rays of the setting sun burnish the platinum setting.

"It's beautiful," she acknowledged, edging around an easel and a basket of wallpaper rolls to be closer to him.

"I might have gotten it in a hurry, but you should

know that I put thought into it." A grin lifted one side of his mouth as she reached his side. "It's kind of intimidating to buy something like this for a fashion designer turned decorator. Undoubtedly, you have very specific tastes when it comes to these things."

"No." She shook her head, certain on that point. Certain also that she liked standing beside him. The scent of his aftershave was muted, but if she inhaled deeply enough, she could catch it.

"Come on." He thumbed the top of the stone. "Design is your life."

"I'm serious. An engagement ring is one item that I'd prefer to be a reflection of how someone sees me. When the day comes that a man gives me such a ring, I will be—" she lifted the ring from his fingers to admire it "—completely dazzled to receive something so uncompromisingly romantic."

Maybe that was part of what hurt about the way he'd told her about the announcement to the media. He hadn't just doled out a gold band for their charade. Her heart had been taunted by this utterly perfect sparkler.

"Well, I know the way you received it was a far cry from romantic." He cast a wary glance her way. "But when I was seized by the idea of an engagement, I saw this ring in my head immediately and shoved my PR coordinator out the door to find it. So if the look of it means anything to you, I'm going to take full credit."

"I really like it. I'm sorry that didn't come across earlier. I think we were both…reeling…reacting…maybe not thinking so much." She closed her fingers around the ring, hiding it from view before handing it back to him. "I hope one day I have something half as beautiful to wear."

He stared at her closed fist and didn't move to take the ring. She could see the wheels turning in his mind and guessed he'd latched on to an idea. Josie felt her stomach flip, not knowing what to expect. Another sales pitch that would break her heart? Or maybe, just maybe, the man who'd picked out this sentimental ring had something else in mind.

"Will you hang on to that for just a minute?" he said suddenly, tugging her toward the love seat. "Just put it in your pocket, okay? Humor me while I try to say something."

Her heart beat faster as she quickened her steps to keep up with him. Reaching for the fearlessness she brought to the work world, she told herself to take a chance on something far more important.

"Actually, I had a few things I wanted to tell you, as well." She sat on the arm of the love seat, too nervous to settle onto the cushion. "I marched out here hoping to catch you so I could come to my own defense about the whole 'maiden in the tower' idea."

"That came out badly," he admitted. "And I apologize. I want the chance to get it right this time."

"I can appreciate what you meant, actually." She did as he asked with the ring, sliding it into a pocket of the cashmere cardigan she'd put on around lunchtime, when she'd decided "comfort clothes" were the order of the day. "I've never been the confrontational type, so I can't sit here and pretend that I wasn't hiding out. I was. However, I would not have hidden for long, and I would have come up with a strategy to deal with the mudslinging that tabloids enjoy so much."

Keith dropped onto the love-seat cushion and faced her.

"They're not slinging mud now, I promise you." His mischievous smile made her curious.

"What do you mean?"

"Go look outside."

Rising, she moved toward the window, wondering how she could get a good look out without them seeing her. Sidling up to a tall archway, she edged her shoulder past the exposed brick and peered straight down.

The cameramen and women were no longer seated on the sidewalk while they waited for a photo op. They were milling around a lamppost out front where a bunch of flowers and stuffed animals were stacked. A handful of young women held homemade signs bearing fat red hearts that said Keith and Josie or Best Wishes, Happy Couple! She could read the big balloon-style letters from here.

"Oh, for crying out loud." Laughing, she didn't know what else to say. "Do you believe that? They'll be so disappointed when—"

"Don't." He covered her lips with one finger, shushing her. "Don't jinx our relationship by saying that out loud."

"Mmph?" she mumbled, until he moved his finger aside. "How do you know what I was going to say?"

"I'm starting to know you pretty well."

"It's been an intense courtship, hasn't it?" She couldn't believe she'd met him just four days ago, or was it three since the wee hours after the engagement party?

"Until tonight, I enjoyed every second." He smoothed her hair behind one shoulder, his fingers lingering on her back. Stroking. "But what else were you going to tell me when you came out here? You said I should have let you handle the publicity problem."

"Actually, I was going to address the maiden in the tower issue, remember?"

"I really pissed you off with that one, didn't I?"

She shook her head, wanting to make herself clear. She might be nonconfrontational, but she could be direct and assertive.

"I just wanted to point out that your mom has a tower of her own, a haven in that big house by the sea."

Keith frowned. "You mean her office?"

"I mean her *haven*," Josie repeated, wondering how a man who'd picked out such a romantic ring could have missed the significance of the highly personalized space Colleen Murphy had created for herself. "Not everyone can deal with the world by wrestling it to the ground with their bare hands, and that's okay. People like me—like your mother—are more subtle. Introverts, maybe. But that doesn't mean we can't kick ass in our own way."

"Having been successfully beaten down by my mom on a few memorable occasions, I know what you mean."

Eyeing her expression, he hastened to add, "Not literally, obviously. But you know, mom maneuvered."

Josie smiled. "Having been ignored by my mother for most of my life, I have no idea. But I'll take your word for it."

He turned her to face him full on, both hands cupping her shoulders. "Josie, I lost the Wholesome Branding account today, before I released the news of our engagement."

"You're kidding." She felt blindsided, so she could only imagine how he felt. "That partnership with them was going to be so huge for you."

"Yeah, it was." He didn't appear as remorseful as she would have thought.

"Wait. You released the engagement news, knowing your work with them was no longer possible?" Confused, she tried to make sense of why he'd gone ahead with a fictional-fiancée story.

"I honestly wasn't doing it to make nice with a potential partner. I'm not changing who I am for the sake of anyone I do business with." He snaked his hands under her hair to cradle the back of her neck, his thumbs rubbing lightly over the base of her scalp. "My main goals still applied, since I wanted to protect both our businesses and put our relationship on safer terrain, where we wouldn't be nitpicked by the tabloids."

She couldn't believe he hadn't been trying to save his Wholesome Branding deal with the whole charade. It made his goals seem less selfish. More noble.

"Safer terrain." That made a difference, since she

could see the sense of it a little better. "Still, I don't feel comfortable living a lie."

Even though the gorgeous ring was practically burning a hole in her pocket.

"I understand." He leaned closer, brushing the softest whisper of a kiss over her temple.

Her knees almost buckled from the sweetness of the gesture. His hand trailed down her arm, smoothing the cashmere over her skin until he reached her bare hand and slid lower, lower.

Into her pocket.

"Josie?" He pulled the ring out and held it up. "You're the most compelling, sexy, principled woman I've ever met."

Her heart caught in her throat. What on earth was he doing?

Rolling the diamond band back and forth between his thumb and forefinger, he forged on. "This is a *dating* ring for someone who rocks my world. Someone I want to know a whole lot better. Would you do me the great honor of wearing this ring that says you're mine exclusively for as long as you like?" The sincerity in his eyes wasn't about putting on a show for the media.

She was a thousand percent positive. The look there said he wanted her for far more than a fling.

"A dating ring?" She had to bite her lip to halt a huge grin from spreading across her face. Unsuccessful, she let him see exactly how delighted this idea made her. "You realize you're really raising the bar for the bachelors in this town?"

He shrugged. "I've worked too hard to deny myself beautiful things."

His green eyes were all for her, and she felt the compliment to her toes.

"You know the rest of the world is going to think the ring means a whole lot more." She'd tried to play by the rules her whole life, in an effort to set herself apart from her parents' slippery morality. How would she feel about being part of so much pretense?

"Good. Maybe they'll leave us alone, so we can enjoy getting to know each other, instead of trying to tear us down by digging into pasts that don't matter." Keith took her hand, but instead of holding up the ring, he pulled her to him. "What do you say? You and me against the world, sharing a big secret?"

"When you put it that way, it sounds as if we'll have the privacy we had on the boat. Just us."

"And we really liked that, didn't we?" His words rumbled in her ear, which was pressed to his chest. He made her breathless, having him this close, and she knew she would be ten kinds of a fool to say no to him.

"I would love to wear your dating ring, Keith Murphy." Josie tipped her chin up to look him in the eye so he'd know just how much it meant to her. "I would savor our secret every day that I looked at it, and cherish the time to get to know you, without the world interfering in our private business."

Her heart was pounding, the vows felt so solemn, so significant. From the way his eyes burned into hers, she knew he felt the same.

Wordlessly, he lifted her hand and slid the princess-cut diamond into place, the fit as flawless as the stone. He centered the setting on her finger before pressing his lips to her knuckles, silently sealing the deal.

"You've made me a very happy man," he whispered, squeezing her palm for a long minute before he kissed his way up her arm to her shoulder. Her neck. "But I've gotta confess I have every intention of making sure that ring never comes off."

In the fading twilight, Josie saw the man in front of her more clearly than she'd ever seen anyone. And she knew he was a rock-solid match for her—honest and hardworking, ambitious yet romantic. If an occasional moment of arrogance crept in, she wasn't going to hold that against him. Especially when he treated her so well it brought tears to her eyes.

"Well, I have news for you, Murphy. This ring isn't going anywhere." She arched up on her toes to kiss his cheek, inhale the masculine scent that she knew would turn her on for the rest of her days. "Besides, you're the prince who rescued me from the tower with audacity and Chinese food, so I think you've won my heart fair and square."

"Prince?" He pulled her hips to his, obviously ready to seal the bargain in another way. "I thought I was the marauding pirate."

He captured her lips in a teasing kiss, his palms covering her butt and lifting her right...

There.

Desire rocked through her, accompanied by so many other emotions.

"Well, it looks like an all-new fantasy plays out here tonight." She scrabbled for better positioning, wrapping her arms tight around his neck to anchor herself where she wanted to be.

"Do I get a sword?" he asked, carrying her toward the living quarters at the back of the loft.

"You feel well armed to me." She wriggled her hips meaningfully.

"I like this game." He kissed her deeply and slowly, pausing just long enough to get his bearings on their way to the bedroom.

"Mmm. I'm glad." She brought his hand to her mouth and kissed his fingers purposefully. "Because I'm dying to reward you properly."

He picked up his pace toward the bed. "And I can't wait to be of service...."

* * * * *

Harlequin® *Blaze*™

COMING NEXT MONTH

Available October 25, 2011

#645 THE SURVIVOR
Men Out of Uniform
Rhonda Nelson

#646 MODEL MARINE
Uniformly Hot!
Candace Havens

#647 THE MIGHTY QUINNS: DANNY
The Mighty Quinns
Kate Hoffmann

#648 INTOXICATING
Lori Wilde

#649 ROPED IN
The Wrong Bed
Crystal Green

#650 ROYALLY CLAIMED
A Real Prince
Marie Donovan

REQUEST YOUR FREE BOOKS!
2 FREE NOVELS PLUS 2 FREE GIFTS!

Harlequin *Blaze*

red-hot reads!

YES! Please send me 2 FREE Harlequin® Blaze™ novels and my 2 FREE gifts (gifts are worth about $10). After receiving them, if I don't wish to receive any more books, I can return the shipping statement marked "cancel." If I don't cancel, I will receive 6 brand-new novels every month and be billed just $4.49 per book in the U.S. or $4.96 per book in Canada. That's a saving of at least 14% off the cover price. It's quite a bargain. Shipping and handling is just 50¢ per book in the U.S. and 75¢ per book in Canada.* I understand that accepting the 2 free books and gifts places me under no obligation to buy anything. I can always return a shipment and cancel at any time. Even if I never buy another book, the two free books and gifts are mine to keep forever.

151/351 HDN FEQE

Name _____ (PLEASE PRINT)

Address _____ Apt. #

City _____ State/Prov. _____ Zip/Postal Code

Signature (if under 18, a parent or guardian must sign)

Mail to the **Reader Service**:
IN U.S.A.: P.O. Box 1867, Buffalo, NY 14240-1867
IN CANADA: P.O. Box 609, Fort Erie, Ontario L2A 5X3

Not valid for current subscribers to Harlequin Blaze books.

Want to try two free books from another line?
Call 1-800-873-8635 or visit www.ReaderService.com.

* Terms and prices subject to change without notice. Prices do not include applicable taxes. Sales tax applicable in N.Y. Canadian residents will be charged applicable taxes. Offer not valid in Quebec. This offer is limited to one order per household. All orders subject to credit approval. Credit or debit balances in a customer's account(s) may be offset by any other outstanding balance owed by or to the customer. Please allow 4 to 6 weeks for delivery. Offer available while quantities last.

Your Privacy—The Reader Service is committed to protecting your privacy. Our Privacy Policy is available online at www.ReaderService.com or upon request from the Reader Service.

We make a portion of our mailing list available to reputable third parties that offer products we believe may interest you. If you prefer that we not exchange your name with third parties, or if you wish to clarify or modify your communication preferences, please visit us at www.ReaderService.com/consumerschoice or write to us at Reader Service Preference Service, P.O. Box 9062, Buffalo, NY 14269. Include your complete name and address.

HBI1B

Harlequin® Special Edition® is thrilled to present a new installment in USA TODAY *bestselling author RaeAnne Thayne's reader-favorite miniseries,* THE COWBOYS OF COLD CREEK.

Join the excitement as we meet the Bowmans—four siblings who lost their parents but keep family ties alive in Pine Gulch. First up is Trace. Only two things get under this rugged lawman's skin: beautiful women and secrets. And in Rebecca Parsons, he finds both!

Read on for a sneak peek of CHRISTMAS IN COLD CREEK. *Available November 2011 from Harlequin® Special Edition®.*

On impulse, he unfolded himself from the bar stool. "Need a hand?"

"Thank you! I…" She lifted her gaze from the floor to his jeans and then raised her eyes. When she identified him her hazel eyes turned from grateful to unfriendly and cold, as if he'd somehow thrown the broken glasses at her head.

He also thought he saw a glimmer of panic in those interesting depths, which instantly stirred his curiosity like cream swirling through coffee.

"I've got it, Officer. Thank you." Her voice was several degrees colder than the whirl of sleet outside the windows.

Despite her protests, he knelt down beside her and began to pick up shards of broken glass. "No problem. Those trays can be slippery."

This close, he picked up the scent of her, something fresh and flowery that made him think of a mountain meadow on a July afternoon. She had a soft, lush mouth and for one brief, insane moment, he wanted to push aside that stray lock of hair slipping from her ponytail and taste her. Apparently he needed to spend a lot less time working and a great deal *more* time recreating with the opposite sex if he could have sudden random fantasies about a woman he wasn't even inclined to like, pretty or not.

"I'm Trace Bowman. You must be new in town."

She didn't answer immediately and he could almost see the wheels turning in her head. Why the hesitancy? And why that little hint of unease he could see clouding the edge of her gaze? His presence was obviously making her uncomfortable and Trace couldn't help wondering why.

"Yes. We've been here a few weeks."

"Well, I'm just up the road about four lots, in the white house with the cedar shake roof, if you or your daughter need anything." He smiled at her as he picked up the last shard of glass and set it on her tray.

Definitely a story there, he thought as she hurried away. He just might need to dig a little into her background to find out why someone with fine clothes and nice jewelry, and who so obviously didn't have experience as a waitress, would be here slinging hash at The Gulch. Was she running away from someone? A bad marriage?

So…Rebecca Parsons. Not Becky. An intriguing woman. It had been a long time since one of those had crossed his path here in Pine Gulch.

Trace won't rest until he finds out Rebecca's secret, but will he still have that same attraction to her once he does? Find out in CHRISTMAS IN COLD CREEK. Available November 2011 from Harlequin® Special Edition®.